My Real

Stacy was in my room. She was leaning over my bed. I stood in the doorway with my eyes nearly bugging out of my head. She had my diary in her hand. She was in the act of putting it back on my mattress and covering it with my pillow.

'Stacy!' I gasped. 'What are you doing?'

She almost jumped out of her shoes at the sound of my voice. She spun around and stared at me. She had the weirdest expression on her face. I couldn't tell whether she looked guilty or angry or upset or just plain startled – or all four of them at once!

'Did you take my diary?' I asked.

She stared at me. She opened her mouth then closed it again without speaking.

I could feel my checks flushing. 'You *know* I never let anyone read my diary,' I said. I felt really shocked.

'Yes,' Stacy said in a strange croaky voice. 'And now I know why.'

Check out some of the other great books
in the Stacy and Friends series

Stacy AND Friends

My Real
Best Friend

Allan Frewin Jones

Series created by Ben M. Baglio

RED FOX

A Red Fox Book

Published by Random House Children's Books
20 Vauxhall Bridge Road, London SW1V 2SA

A division of Random House UK Ltd
London Melbourne Sydney Auckland
Johannesburg and agencies throughout the world

This edition 1998

1 3 5 7 9 10 8 6 4 2

Printed and bound in Great Britain by
Cox & Wyman Ltd, Reading, Berkshire

Papers used by Random House UK Limited
are natural, recyclable products made from wood grown in
sustainable forests. The manufacturing processes conform to
the environmental regulations of the country of origin.

RANDOM HOUSE UK Limited Reg. No. 954009

ISBN 0 09 9263629

Have you ever seen one of those programmes on TV where they set up these therapy sessions for people with real bad problems?

In the programmes I've seen, all the people with *real bad problems* sit in a circle with a professional therapy-type guy at one end. (Yes, I know circles don't have ends – I guess I meant at one point in the circle, OK?)

Then all the people with RBPs (that's short for Real Bad Problems) stand up one at a time and introduce themselves and say what their real bad problem is.

OK, picture me in one of those sessions. It's a meeting of LBA, which stands for Little Brothers Anonymous.

It's my turn to stand up. I stand up. Everyone looks at me.

'Hi, my name's Cindy, and I have a real bad problem.'

'Hi, Cindy.' (That's the therapist speaking.)

1

'Would you like to tell us all what your real bad problem is, please?'

'My real bad problem is that I have the WORST LITTLE BROTHERS IN THE ENTIRE UNIVERSE!'

'I think you'll find that isn't the case, Cindy,' says the therapist. 'If you'd like to tell us about your little brothers, I think you'll find everyone here has had similar problems.'

'OK,' I say. 'I'll tell you about Denny and Bob, my seven-year-old twin brothers!'

'Tell us *everything*, Cindy,' says the therapist. 'Don't leave anything out.'

'Darn right I will!'

I start to tell them about my twin brothers.

We stop for lunch. Then I carry on explaining about Denny and Bob through the afternoon. We stop for dinner. The sun goes down. We go to bed. Next day I continue to tell them all how awful Denny and Bob are.

Three days later, when I finally finish telling them about the horrible things that Denny and Bob do, they all agree with me that Denny and Bob are definitely, absolutely, positively, completely, totally and utterly the WORST LITTLE BROTHERS IN THE ENTIRE UNIVERSE.

Everyone looks really sympathetic. I sit down.

It's the next person's turn, but after what I've been telling them, the other people all decide things aren't so bad for them after all, and they all go home, feeling much better about their lives.

I go home, too. Denny and Bob are hiding behind the front door with water pistols filled with grape juice.

Have you ever been squirted with grape juice by two people at once? You get sticky. You get very sticky indeed.

I hate being sticky.

I hate my twin brothers.

I even put a notice up on the board at school.

Urgent!
Home required for lively seven-year-old twin
boys.
They answer to the names Denny and Bob.
If your life is becoming dull and predictable
this could be just the thing you need!
Excitement! Thrills! Surprises! More thrills!
All reasonable offers considered for immediate
delivery. (Sorry – no returns.)
Contact Cindy Spiegel.
Quickly, please!
Urgent!
Very URGENT!

I didn't get any takers. I guess I'm stuck with them.

Maybe you think I'm exaggerating about them? Maybe you're thinking, hey, they can't be all THAT bad.

Wanna bet?

My very best friend in all the world is Stacy Allen. We're both ten, which, if you ask me, is a pretty neat age to be. Like, you're old enough to *know* about boys, but not so old that you go totally *goofy* when one of them talks to you. Stacy and I have made a pact that if ever either of us starts going goofy about boys, the other one will point it out and put a stop to it. I can't honestly imagine it'll ever be necessary, but you can never tell. There are thirteen-year-old girls at our school who are total *dorks* when it comes to boys.

Stacy is smaller than me, but that's because her growth spurt hasn't quite kicked in yet. She has straight dark brown hair which she hates. She says she'd like wavy auburn hair like mine. I've told her I'd swap if I *could*. Anyway, I think straight brown hair can be really neat – like with Jewel de Monteville in *Spindrift*. (*Spindrift* is our fave daytime soap – more about that later.)

Stacy also has freckles, which drives her crazy. I don't have freckles. I don't have a teeth-brace either, but I don't talk about that, because Stacy is kind of sensitive about hers.

Anyway, like I keep telling her, looks aren't all that much! I mean, Stacy is a whole heap smarter than I am. In fact, where coming up with real neat plans and brilliant solutions to problems, and mega-superb advice is concerned, Stacy is the best friend a person could ever want. And she's funny, too.

Like I said, Stacy is my all-time best friend ever, but I do have two other really close friends: Pippa Kane and Fern Kipsak. But when the stuff I'm going to tell you about started, Pippa and Fern weren't around.

Stacy and I were in my living room. We'd staked out the couch because it was time for *Spindrift*. A very special episode of *Spindrift*. The climax to a story that had been building up for *weeks*.

I really don't have time to explain everything, but what happened was that Kurt Freeman's boatyard had been in financial trouble because his partner and best pal, Jake Russell, had vanished after clearing out their joint bank account. (Oh yeah, and Jake took Kurt's wife, Cecilia, too, but she was a total nightmare, so that was no big deal, although Kurt was upset about it for some reason. He was better off without her, if you ask me.)

5

Anyway, Kurt had put his racing yacht, *Spindrift*, into a big prestigious race, but he needed some cash quick to fit the yacht up. So he borrowed some money off the Mob. It got really complicated after that, but the point is that at the end of the last episode, a contract killer with the Mob, Bert 'Snake-eyes' O'Hara, had kidnapped Kurt's teenage daughter, Abby, and had taken her to a deserted ocean-front cabin and threatened to wipe her out if Kurt didn't pay back the money, like, *immediately*. The race was nearly over, and the only way Kurt was going to be able to pay back the Mob's money was if he won the race with *Spindrift*.

Kurt was neck and neck with his big rival, Max Landower, in his yacht, *Golden Dawn*. But Jake had planted a bomb on *Spindrift* which was set to explode in, like, two minutes, so that he could pick up the insurance on the yacht. *Also*, Kurt's wife was about to discover that Jake was already married and that his secret wife was the brains behind the biggest diamond robbery on the West Coast *ever*, and that her (Cecilia's) luggage (for their vacation to South America) was stuffed with the diamonds. You see, he didn't want *her* (Cecilia) at all – he just wanted to use her as a courier to get the diamonds out of the country – in her

6

luggage! At the end of the previous episode, Cecilia's luggage was about to be searched at the airport.

Phew! Got all that? Pretty *frantic* stuff, huh?

Basically, this was *the* episode! If things went haywire, Kurt could wind up blown to pieces, Abby could get shot and Cecilia could spend the next twenty-five years behind bars.

So, let's be honest here, Stacy and I were kind of *looking forward* to this episode. We didn't want to miss a single moment.

Denny and Bob had other ideas.

The *Spindrift* credits rolled. Stacy and I were on the edge of the couch cushions. We would hardly eat our caramel popcorn, we were so tense. There was the usual shot of *Spindrift*, cresting the waves with Kurt at the helm and Abby waving from the bow.

Starring Brad Rainshaw as Kurt Freeman
Deke Lancaster as Jake Russell
Jewel de Monteville as Cecilia Freeman
Bootsie Morgan as Abby Freeman
Mitch Louis Hopkins as . . . .

Yes! Yes! Get on with it!

The episode opened in the dark cabin where Abby was being held at gunpoint.

'Oww!' Stacy yelled. A ball had bounced off

the back of her neck. She glared over the back of the couch. 'Denny'n'Bob. I know that was you! Quit it!' (Stacy can't tell the twins apart, so she always calls them 'Denny'n'Bob', as if they just have the one joint name between them.)

'Ignore them,' I said.

Stacy frowned at me. She rubbed her head. 'That's easy for you to say,' she told me.

There were giggles from out in the hall.

On screen there was a gunshot!

Bang!

'Ohmigosh, he shot her!' gasped Stacy.

A beachball came sailing over the back of the couch. It hit our mega-bucket of popcorn and sent the whole thing flying over the carpet like a yellow snowstorm!

Denny and Bob were giggling their stupid heads off from behind the cover of the archway into the hall.

I did my very best quit-it-or-die glare in their direction. 'Get out of here!' I shrieked. 'If you imbeciles throw just one more thing in this room I'm gonna make you eat it!'

More giggles.

Snorting with irritation, I turned again to the TV.

It was a totally different scene! We were on the yacht. Kurt was trying to defuse the bomb. 'What happened?' I shrieked at Stacy. 'Did she get shot?'

'I don't know, I missed it. There was pop-corn flying everywhere.'

'I don't believe this!' I yelled. 'I'm going to kill them!'

'Wait until after the show,' Stacy said, 'and I'll help you.'

'Nyahh-nyahh-nyah!' Denny and Bob had come out of hiding and were dancing up and down in the doorway, pulling faces and making stupid noises.

I'd just like to mention at this point that one of the real problems I have with my little broth-ers, apart from them being a total nightmare, is that they have these totally sweet, innocent faces. They can do big-eyed I-didn't-do-it expressions that would make Bambi look like a hardened criminal. They can get away with close to murder, I'm telling you!

But right now, the pair of them looked like a couple of little *fiends*, sticking their tongues out and kicking up such a racket that we could hardly hear the TV.

I tried threats.

'If you don't get lost, I'm going to *kill* you!'

'Nyahh-nyahh-na-nahh-nyahh!'

I tried bribery.

'There's some chocolate ice cream in the freezer. Your favourite!'

9

'NYAHH-NYAHH!'

I tried diplomacy.

I leaned over the back of the couch. 'Look, guys, just leave us alone for half an hour, huh? *Please?*'

'No way!' said Bob. 'You got us grounded!'

'What was I supposed to do?' I yelled. 'Not tell Mom that there was strawberry jam down the back of the stereo? The darned thing could have blown up next time it was turned on!'

'You didn't have to tell on us!' shouted Denny.

'You shouldn't have been in here with food, anyway,' I yelled back. 'You know that!'

'Nyahhh!'

'Oh, smart reply, Bob,' I said. 'Have you hired a new scriptwriter?'

Squirt!

'Arrgh!' I got a face full of water.

'Smart enough for ya?' Denny laughed.

I didn't even see where the water pistol had come from. Suddenly it was in Bob's hand and he did a big, long squirt clear across the room.

'Eeeee-yyyyowwwww-oooogh!' Stacy screamed as the cold water went down the back of her neck.

That did it!

I guess the sensible thing would have been to treat them with the contempt they deserved,

10

but it is kind of difficult to ignore a face full of cold water, especially when you know there's plenty more of it to come. One thing about Denny and Bob – when they decide to be *pests*, they're good enough at it to win a gold medal at the Pest Olympics.

Stacy looked fit to kill.

The sooner we dealt with the terrible twins, the quicker we could get back to *Spindrift*.

There was a big explosion from the TV.

I snapped my head around. Had the bomb gone off? It sure looked like it. There was a lot of smoke billowing up, and bits of what looked like it had been a boat a few seconds back were raining down into the water.

I glared at Denny and Bob. 'Kill!' I screamed.

'KILL!' Stacy screamed.

We dived at Denny and Bob.

They ran.

Denny scooted upstairs with Stacy in hot, murderous pursuit.

Bob ran into the kitchen and we played tag around the table.

'Can't catch me!' he was yelling.

He skipped out through the door and headed back down the hall. I was only a couple of inches behind him.

He was heading for the front door!

11

I couldn't let him escape.

Suddenly the front door opened. I saw Dad standing there with his arms full of stuff. A look of surprise and shock went over Dad's face as he saw Bob hurtling towards him with his head down.

Next thing, Bob had crashed into him. All the stuff went flying out of Dad's arms. Bob bounced off Dad.

From the living room I heard a voice on the TV.

'Mrs Freeman? Mrs Cecilia Freeman? I have a warrant here to arrest you for grand larceny. You need not say anything, but anything you do say will be . . .'

Argh! Abby had been shot. (Possibly!) Kurt had been blown up! (Probably!) and Cecilia was being arrested for possession of stolen diamonds! And thanks to my super-pest brothers, I'D MISSED EVERYTHING!

'It wasn't *me*!' Bob yelled. Dad just stood there, surrounded by all the stuff that he'd dropped when Bob had crashed into him. My dad isn't the sort of person who gets instantly mad. He takes his time, and then he gets good and mad!

'Cindy was chasing me!' Bob hollered.

'Why?' Dad asked calmly.

'For nuffin'!'

'For totally ruining it while I was trying to watch *Spindrift*!' I said. 'They were throwing balls and squirting water and everything.'

'I did not!' howled Bob.

Dad pointed to the dripping water pistol in Bob's hand. 'What's that?' he asked.

Bob whipped it behind his back. 'Nuffin'.'

'Why were you annoying your sister?' Dad asked.

'I wasn't.'

'They were getting back at me because of the strawberry jam,' I said. 'Like it was my fault!'

There were yells and stampeding noises from upstairs. Denny came whooshing down the stairs, laughing his head off. He came to a screeching halt when he saw Dad. He put on his innocent face and backed off. Stacy flew down the stairs and crunched right into him.

'Oww! You stupid great ape,' she yelled. 'I'm going to beat you to de-*oh*! Oh, hi, Mr Spiegel.'

'She started it!' Denny said, pointing at Stacy. 'She started chasing me for no reason.'

'Is that a fact?' Dad said. 'Well, since none of you seems to have anything better to do, you can all help me carry this stuff through to the kitchen. How does that sound?'

'But Dad,' I began, '*Spindrift*!'

'I don't see you watching it right now, Cindy,' he said. 'If you have time to chase your brothers around the house, I'm sure you have time to help me out. Huh?'

I decided pretty quickly that it was probably better to go along with him rather than stand there arguing about it, especially as arguments with my dad always wind up the same way: Dad wins! And it wasn't like there was tons of stuff to carry. At least, that was what I thought.

I started picking stuff up. There was a tennis racket and a pair of old golfing shoes. There was a baseball mitt and a bunch of ancient

National Geographic magazines tied up with string. There was a fondue maker still in its box and there was a collection of barbecue skewers. Also, there were a few old sweaters and jumpers and a baseball cap with 'I'M THE MAN' written on it.

Stacy came and helped. I knew she was thinking the same as me: the quicker we get this over with, the quicker we can be back in front of the TV.

Dad looked at the twins. 'Well?' he said.

They joined in.

'Oh, and by the way,' Dad said, 'you two are grounded for an extra two days for annoying your sister.'

'Aw, but –' the twins screeched in chorus.

'Do you want to make it an extra four days?' Dad asked.

Denny and Bob both shut up.

Dad went back outside. 'There's plenty more out here for you to help with,' he called.

I took a look. Jeepers! The front drive was *stacked* with junk! We were going to be all *night* with this. We were going to miss every single second of *Spindrift*. And it was all down to my horrible little brothers!

'I'm going to get you for this,' Bob hissed at me while Dad was out of earshot. 'We're grounded two extra days thanks to you!'

15

'You're going to get *me*?' I whispered back. 'I'm going to get *you*!'

'Yeah?' said Denny. 'You and whose army?'

'I don't need an army, twerp!' I said. 'I can deal with you all on my own!'

'You won't be on your own,' whispered Stacy.

'Ooh!' Bob said sarcastically. 'Big scary Stacy!'

Dad stuck his head in the hall. 'Any problems, guys?' he asked. 'Do I hear bickering going on?'

'Nope,' I said. 'No problems. No bickering.'

'Excellent,' Dad said.

We resorted to deadly glares from then on.

I guess I should explain exactly where all that strange stuff out in our drive actually came from.

It came from our garage.

My dad had been clearing out our garage for the past two weeks. He'd been *talking* about clearing out our garage for two months, and he said he'd been *thinking* about it for, like two *years*.

I could understand why he needed a long run-up to it. My pal Pippa said that cleaning out our garage was the equivalent to the twelve labours of Hercules all rolled into one. Pippa's mom is a college professor, so Pippa knows about stuff like that.

'What were the twelve labours of Hercules, then?' I asked her.

Pippa spent a long time frowning and thinking. 'I don't remember all of them,' she said. 'But he had to do something with the gabardine swines.'

'Gabardine?' Stacy asked. 'Isn't that stuff you make coats out of?'

'Maybe,' Pippa said guardedly, like she wasn't sure.

'So, these gabardine swines were pigs in coats, then?' Fern said, with a grin. 'Is that it?'

'Possibly,' Pippa said. 'I don't exactly remember.'

'So, what did he have to do with them?' I asked.

'I don't remember,' Pippa sighed. I could tell she was wishing she'd never mentioned the twelve labours of Hercules. 'But another of his tasks was to clean out some really filthy stables, I remember *that*.'

'That sounds more like it,' I said. 'How did he do it?'

'Uh, he diverted a river so it went right through the stables and washed everything out.'

I imagined a river flooding through our garage. Yeah, that'd do the job.

'Didn't the horses get washed away?' Stacy asked. Stacy is really into animals, so she would worry about that.

'No. He moved them first,' Pippa said.

'Time out!' Fern said. 'If these labours of Hercules were such a big deal, how come they weren't in the movie?'

Pippa snorted. 'The movie wasn't the *real* story of Hercules!' she said. 'It was all just made up.'

'I thought the whole thing was made up,' Stacy said. 'Hercules is just a legend, Pippa. Legends aren't real.'

'Yes, but . . .' Pippa frowned and did some more thinking. 'The *real* legend was made up thousands of years ago, but the movie story was only made up recently. *That's* the difference. Now, can we please talk about something else?'

That's Pippa for you. I never did find out what Hercules was meant to do with the pigs in coats, but it all sounds a little odd if you ask me, even for a legend. Pigs in coats? Is Pippa crazy or what?

Anyway, like I was saying, my dad had been messing around in the garage on and off for the past two weeks, and all the stuff he had in his arms when Denny walloped into him was what he'd retrieved from out there.

It was quite funny: Dad was dividing the garage junk into three types: stuff we could sell in a yard sale, stuff we needed to take to the dump, and the stuff that he thought shouldn't be in the garage in the first place.

Every now and then he'd come into the house in triumph with something and say: 'Hey, Maggie,'(that's my mom) 'look what I found!' And it would be a hideous old fishing hat or some ancient vinyl albums by a rock group no one had ever heard of, or a half-finished model of some airplane or other. And he'd say, 'I don't know how that got out there, I've been looking for it for ages! Lucky I found it, huh?'

And I could tell from the expression on my mom's face, that she'd hidden that stuff out there on purpose. And then Dad would go around for days with the horrible hat on, and play the horrible old music albums over and over, and take up three-quarters of the kitchen table with the bits of the model airplane.

Mom took me to one side and said: '*This* is what men are like, honey. Little boys don't grow up – it's just that their toys get more expensive!'

I wasn't sure exactly what she meant, but I wrote it down as an Interesting Quote in my Secret Diary.

(I'd tell you all about my Secret Diary, but I'm afraid it's a total, utter and complete secret. No one ever, *ever* gets to read *any* of it. Ever! Sorry.)

Well, it took around twenty minutes to shift everything off the front drive. The kitchen was totally stuffed. Stacy and I raced into the living room to catch the end of *Spindrift*.

The end credits were flashing by at super-speed, like they do.

Then the stupid woman announcer came on screen, grinning all over her stupid face.

'Wow! Wasn't that great?' she said. Gri-i-i-in. 'Watch out for a whole new bunch of story-lines and some brand-new characters in next Monday's episode of *Spindrift*!'

'Arrrgh!' I screamed.

'Arrrgh!' Stacy screamed.

'What's the problem, girls?' Mom asked. She had just walked in through the front door. She has a really high-powered job, and she often doesn't get in until late. She came into the living room and threw herself down in the arm-chair. 'Rats,' she said, looking at the TV. 'I just missed it!' She smiled at us. 'Well, come on girls, tell me all about it. What happened?'

'ARRRGH!'

It was my mom's turn to go 'Arrrgh!' ten

minutes later when she saw all the junk that Dad had made us move in out of the garage. 'What have you done to the kitchen?' she wailed.

'It's OK, honey,' I heard Dad say. 'It's mostly for the yard sale. We'll make big bucks, trust me.'

'What's it all doing in *here*?' Mom asked. (A reasonable question, I thought.)

'I have to sort it all and price it all and label it all,' Dad said.

Mom came stalking out of the kitchen. 'I'm going to take a bath,' she called. 'I want my kitchen back by the time I finish!'

I looked at Stacy. She looked at me. We were both thinking the same thing. More hard labour! Uh-oh! Time to make ourselves scarce.

We zipped up to my room.

'My dad always has *ideas*,' I said gloomily, once we were safely hidden away up there. 'It drives my mom crazy.'

Stacy grinned. 'I like people who have ideas,' she said. 'It makes life more interesting.'

'I guess,' I said. I wasn't entirely convinced. Life with my family could certainly be described as interesting, but sometimes I could have used a little *dullness*, know what I mean? Just to make a change.

'Actually,' I said, brightening up, 'I had an idea recently. A really, really great idea.'

'Yeah?' Stacy asked. 'What?'

I made the locked-lips sign. 'It's a surprise,' I said. 'A super-secret surprise.' I grinned at her. 'But you'll love it!'

'Tell me!' said Stacy.

'Nope! Not yet. Just be patient,' I told her. 'It'll be worth waiting for. It's totally *wonderful*.'

It was, too.

Stunningly wonderful!

3

Puff! Puff-puff-puff! Pu-u-u-u-uff!

Gasp!

Pu-u-u-u-u-u-uff!

Gasp, gasp!

Squeee-eee-eege.

'Quick,' I yelled to Stacy. 'Put your finger over the valve, the air's escaping again!'

'I . . . can't . . . do . . . this . . .' Stacy panted. 'I'm . . . going . . . dizzy . . .'

'You're nearly there,' I said. 'Just a few more times should do it.' I tested the air mattress. Yeah, just a few more lungfuls of air and it would be nice and firm.

I *would* have helped Stacy inflate the mattress, but that kind of thing makes my ears pop, and I really *hate* that. So I was giving Stacy all the encouragement she could possibly need to make up for not actually *helping* her.

She took a deep breath and started puffing at the valve again.

It would have made things a whole lot easier

23

if the hose part of the darned pump hadn't been missing. It had definitely been there when I'd put the pump away last. You know, if I was a *suspicious* type of person, I might suspect that someone had deliberately *taken* the hose part of the pump just to make it really hard work for us to inflate Stacy's mattress next time she slept over! Like, for instance, a pair of totally pestilential twins! (I got the word 'pestilential' from Pippa – she said it's a really impressive way of saying 'pesky'.)

The problem was that we didn't find out that a piece of the pump was missing until pretty late, and by then my beastly brothers were tucked up in bed. And since Stacy and I should have been in bed – like, two hours ago – as well, we couldn't really go and complain to my folks.

'Did you know you go cross-eyed when you blow hard?' I asked Stacy.

'Splug-hhhaaahhhgh!' She nearly blew a gasket laughing. 'Cindy! You're not helping!' she choked. 'Don't say stuff like that when I'm in mid-blow!'

Schbloooooze went the air mattress.

'Finger!' I said. 'Valve!'

She put her finger over the valve.

'I feel like my head's going to explode,' she moaned. She tested the mattress with her free hand. 'That'll do,' she said. 'I'm out of air!' She screwed the top onto the valve.

'Are you sure it's full enough?' I asked.

Stacy stretched out on the mattress. She sank into it like a rock in a soufflé. 'It's fine,' she said. 'I can hardly feel the floor at all.' We looked at each other and both started to giggle.

There was a knock on the door. 'Are you girls in bed yet?' It was Dad.

'Yes,' I called, leaping up onto my bed.

'Good. Sleep tight. Don't lie awake talking all night.'

'We won't,' I called.

'We wouldn't *dream* of it!' called Stacy. 'Honest.'

Dad laughed. He knew what we were like.

We sorted ourselves out and I switched off the main light, so that the only light was the one on my bedside table. My bedside lamp is in the shape of a crescent moon, and it glows really softly and makes everything in the room seem strange and mysterious.

It's a really good light to tell spooky stories by. Sometimes, when our gang has a sleepover party, we sit up for hours telling each other spooky stories. Stacy tells the best ones. She has this really great story about the Monster Sister who spends all the day chained up down in the basement, but who roams the house at night looking for people to eat.

Stacy's Monster Sister is called Amandosaurus. She has tangled white hair, all bunched up on top of her head in a big messy bouffant that's totally full of rats. Ugh! She has long, red fingernails, like claws. And she's pale and ugly and has rotten teeth and really bad breath. I wonder where Stacy got the idea of Amandosaurus from? Could it be her thirteen-year-old real sister, Amanda, at all? I think we should be told!

My monster creatures of the night are two evil little gnomes called Deadhead and Blob.

Pippa's favourite story is 'The Phantom of the Opera'. She does a really good performance of a lunatic playing the organ – which is what the Phantom does when he's not abducting people and dragging them down into the sewers. Fern always tells stories about midnight alien abductions.

The really great thing about Stacy and me is that we both have nightmare families! I mean, I have Denny and Bob, and she has Amanda. That means we can really sympathise about all the terrible things that happen. It's not really the same with Fern and Pippa because neither of them has any brothers and sisters, so it's kind of difficult for them to understand how totally awful if can be.

Hey, I don't want you to think I don't love my little brothers. Of course I do! It's just that I hate them as well, if you know what I mean.

That night, Stacy and I talked for the *longest* time before we fell asleep. In fact, I don't remember falling asleep at all. The last thing I remember was Stacy saying, 'It must be really neat to be a food taster in a chocolate cookie factory.'

The next thing I knew was waking up with a snake in bed with me.

I was dreaming about lizards – *hissy* lizards. Then I felt this cold *thing* against my leg. I nearly shot through the ceiling when I threw the bed covers back and saw the snake.

I was out of bed like a rocket.

'Aiiiieeeeeeeee!' I grabbed a magazine and started beating at the snake with it.

'Gw-gwk-huh?' Stacy blinked at me. 'Hey! What's the big idea!' She sat up on her almost totally deflated mattress. 'Ow!' she said. 'Floor!' she said. 'Hard!'

'*Hisssssss-splut!* That was the last of the air escaping the mattress. No wonder I'd been dreaming of hissing lizards – I must have heard the air hissing out of the mattress in my sleep.

That was when I heard the stifled giggling from outside my bedroom door.

I quit battering the snake to death with my magazine and actually took a look at it. It was made of rubber.

I glared at the door. If I was Supergirl I'd have used my laser beam eyes to burn right through the door and incinerate those two brothers of mine!

They must have sneaked in as soon as they thought we were asleep. They'd pulled the plug on Stacy's mattress and given me a rubber reptile to sleep with. And now they were outside, choking themselves with laughter!

I grabbed the snake and ran for the door. I wanted to see how they'd look with their rubber snake wrapped around their scrawny necks and tied in a really tight knot!

'Yeow! Oww! Yowch! Yewwwch!' I ran right onto sharp stuff in my bare feet. The jerks had scattered the carpet with a whole heap of their little model soldiers. It was as bad as stepping onto tacks!

I head more giggling, and the sound of the pair of them scuttling quietly down the hallway.

Stacy was staring at me as I managed to get clear of the spiky booby trap.

'I'm sorry, but we're going to have to kill them,' I said quite calmly to Stacy.

'Don't be sorry,' she said getting up. 'I'll

help you! Ouch!' She hopped around clutching at her feet. 'Ow!Ow!' They'd bobby-trapped around her mattress with little soldiers as well.

You have to give it to those kids – they work *hard* for their kicks. But the kind of kicks they were about to get from Stacy and me were going to be a little different. A little *harder*.

'What about weapons?' Stacy asked.

I nodded. 'I got it!' I said. 'We can get bottles of shower gel and shampoo from the bathroom. We can squirt them with 'em! And we can get sponges full of cold water to squish over them.'

'Excellently excellent!' Stacy said.

'Keep the noise down, though,' I warned her. 'Mom and Dad will go crazy if they hear us.'

'I know,' Stacy said. 'Amanda and I have learned to fight real quietly.'

We crept into the darkened hall.

We tiptoed to the bathroom and picked up our deadly squirty and soaky weapons. We looked at each other and giggled silently. Those dumb twins wouldn't know what had hit them!

Doing our best not to squeeze too much water out of the sponges, we headed for the twins' room, which was right at the end of the hall past Mom and Dad's room.

I put my mouth right up to Stacy's ear. 'Here's the plan,' I whispered. 'They'll be expecting us, so we need to act real fast if we're going to accomplish our mission.'

'Gotcha,' Stacy whispered back.

'Right. I'll count to three, yeah? Then I'll turn the handle and we both rush in there and let them have it before they know what's hit 'em, right?'

'Check!'

'Ready?'

Stacy got herself into position, drippy sponge in one hand, and a family-size shampoo bottle (for normal to dry hair, in case you were wondering) in the other.

'Ready!'

I mouthed the countdown. 'Three! Two! One!'

I turned the handle and we hurled ourselves at the door.

Crunch! Splat!

The door didn't open! We both splatted smack into it and got soaked by our own sponges.

I knew for sure there was no lock on the inside of the room – the little terrors must have wedged something up against the door handle!

'Nyahh-nyahh! Can't get in!'

I was about to go ballistic when I heard a

faint creaking sound from my parents' bed-room. Someone was awake in there! Oh heck! We'd be found, red-handed out there! (Well, *wet*-handed, anyhow.)

We shot each other a quick glance before high-tailing it back to my room as quickly and as quietly as possible.

The terrors had won! That is, for *now* they had won!

Stacy and I changed into a couple of spare sets of my nightclothes and we both got into my bed. After all, I could hardly let Stacy sleep on the hard floor now that her mattress was flat as a flapjack – and she sure wasn't in the mood to spend half an hour trying to blow it up again.

It was a bit of a tight squeeze, but we just about fit in my bed, so long as neither of us wanted to get really comfortable.

'So,' Stacy said. 'Who has the worst family? You or me?'

'Me!' I said with very deep feeling. 'Denny and Bob are twice as bad as your sister.'

'I'm not so sure', Stacy said. 'Amanda can be pretty horrible when she puts her mind to it.'

'Yeah, but there's only *one* of her,' I pointed out.

'But she's much bigger,' said Stacy. 'And don't forget the other Bimbos.' She was talking

31

about Cheryl and Rachel and Natalie, who, together with Amanda, made up the Bimbo Brigade. (That's what we call them, anyhow. Well, it's only fair – they call us the Nerds, which we definitely are *not*!)

'Well, would you swap Denny'n'Bob for Amanda?' Stacy asked.

I thought about it. 'It couldn't be *worse*,' I said.

'Wanna bet?' Stacy said.

I thought about all the problems that Stacy had with Amanda. Then I thought about how annoying Denny and Bob could be.

'You know what would be really neat?' I said. 'Denny and Bob and Amanda as one family, would be really neat. And then you and I could be sisters. Uh, Stacy, could you move your feet a little, please? It's like sharing the bed with an iceberg!'

'They're cold,' Stacy said. 'I was trying to warm them up on you, is all.'

'You're not making you warm – you're making me cold!'

'Sorry. I usually warm myself up on Benjamin. He makes the perfect hot-water bottle.' Benjamin is Stacy's pet cat. 'But you're right – Amanda and Denny'n'Bob really ought to have to live together. That would be so brilliant!'

'And if we were sisters, we could share a room,' I said.

'A big room,' said Stacy.

'Sure, a huge room!' I agreed. 'With two beds.'

'That would be great!'

'Yeah!'

There was a pause

'Uh, who would get which set of parents?' Stacy asked.

Oh! I hadn't thought of that.

I sure wouldn't want to lose my mom and dad to Amanda and the twins. And I guess Stacy would feel the same.

Rats! Nothing in this life is ever *simple*, is it?

4

I woke up the next morning to the worst day of my entire life.

Of course, when I first opened my eyes that Saturday morning, I didn't know it was going to be the worst day of my entire life. I thought it was going to be a pretty normal kind of day. The plan was that Stacy and I would have breakfast, and then, after a leisurely look at morning TV, we would get a ride to the mall to meet Pippa and Fern.

That was the *plan*.

Things didn't work out quite like that. Something awful happened even before we got around to eating our breakfast.

I mean, when you have a friend who is the best friend you have in the entire world, you don't expect that friend to totally *betray your trust*, do you? And I could even have forgiven her for that, if not for the way she behaved, when . . .

Well, let me explain.

34

I keep a Secret Diary. I told you about that, didn't I? I never, ever let anyone see it. It has all my most personal and private thoughts in it. The way I see it is this: if you're going to write down all your most private thoughts, then the book in which you write them has to be totally off limits to everyone. I mean, *everyone*. For instance, suppose I was really mad at my mom for some reason. I'd want to write that down. But how could I if I knew my mom was going to read what I wrote when I was mad?

Or maybe Fern might really annoy me. (She can be annoying at times.) Rather than have a bad argument with her, I think it's a much better idea to let off steam by writing in my diary exactly what I think of her.

I guess you can see how important it is that no one reads my diary. After all, a person can say, or *write* in my case, some pretty mean things in the heat of the moment when a person is feeling really angry or upset. And those things need to be kept completely secret. Anyone with half a brain could see that.

Stacy was in the bathroom and I was in the living room, leaning over the back of the couch and watching an old *Scooby-Doo* cartoon.

'It's Mr Postlethwaite, the caretaker, in a monster suit!' I yelled at the TV. I'd seen this episode about a dozen times, but I still loved it.

Then I suddenly remembered that I hadn't written my diary entry the previous night.

I only ever write in my diary when I'm alone, so on sleepovers I usually do a double entry the following night. But I wanted to tell my diary exactly how much I hated the twins while my feelings were still fresh.

I zipped upstairs. (Oh, in case you were wondering, I'd dumped all the toy soldiers in an old shoe box and hidden it in the linen closet. It was going to be a rainy day in the Sahara Desert before I was gonna tell Denny and Bob where they were, too! They could just spend the day *searching*.)

I keep my diary under my pillow.

I felt under the pillow.

Huh?

It wasn't there.

I dragged my pillow to one side. Nope, nothing. I groped down between the mattress and the bedhead. Still nothing.

I looked under the bed. I found a sock that had been missing for ages. And I found a favourite pen and a hair grip in the shape of a butterfly. These were all nice things to find, but they didn't make up for having lost my diary.

Then it hit me! The twins!

I raced down the corridor and cannoned into

their room. They were sprawled on the floor, playing one of their kill-'em-all, shoot-first-and-count-the-bodies-later-type computer games.

Brakooom! Budda-budda! Kapoweeeeee! Brooommm!

'Yeah! Yah! Got ya!' Bob screeched. 'Astro-cops rule!'

Bukka-bukka-bukka. Pikowwww. Squeeeka-zipp! Blamoozle!

'Gotcha right back!' Denny howled.

The computer screen was full of violent explosions and uniformed people and green blobby things flying through the air.

'Hey! Where's my diary?' I yelled above the noise.

'Splaargg the Space Mutant Strikes again!' Denny yelled, banging his fingers down on his control pad. 'Death to all earthlings!'

Kaboom!

'Hey! Did you hear me?' I howled. 'What have you done with my diary?'

Denny looked up at me. 'What have you done with our soldiers?'

'They're in a box in the airing cupboard,' I said. 'I want my diary back, now!'

Denny turned back to the screen. 'Splaargg the Space Mutant destroys New York!' he said. New York went *kaboom* on the screen.

'I told you where your soldiers are,' I said. 'You have to tell me where my diary is.' I tried not to sound too frantic. My twin brothers are like a pair of sharks. Once they smell blood in the water they go in for the kill. If they realised how desperate I was to get my diary back, there would be a total feeding frenzy.

Bob looked around at me. 'We don't know where your stupid diary is,' he said. 'We haven't touched your stupid diary.'

Denny came up with one of his innocent looks. 'You can search us, if you don't believe us,' he said. 'You can search the whole room.'

'I will!'

I proceeded to take their room apart. I looked everywhere. I turned the whole place upside down.

'When you find out who really took your diary,' Bob said, while I flung bedclothes around the room from the top bunk, 'you're gonna have to come and put everything back the way it was.'

In their dreams! All I'd done was move the mess around a little. I stared down at them from my perch on Denny's bunk bed. I was pretty breathless by then.

'I'll give you to the count of three,' I gasped. 'Then I'm going to go and tell Mom.'

Bob glared up at me. 'We haven't got your

diary!' he said. 'You just want to get us into more trouble.'

I jumped down. 'No,' I said. 'I don't. I just want my diary back.'

'Cross our hearts and hope to die,' Danny said solemnly. 'We haven't got your diary.'

I looked at them. Grr! They looked so darned innocent! It was infuriating. How could two such horrible little beasts have such angelic faces?

Or could I be wrong? Maybe my diary had slipped down the back of the mattress and *under* it somehow. You know, between the mattress and the base of the bed? I hadn't actually looked there. Maybe I had kind of jumped to conclusions. (It's an easy thing to do when you share a house with the terrible twosome!)

I marched out of their room. I'd have one final *thorough* search all around my bed and then, if they didn't cough my diary up in, like, five seconds, I'd go and tell Mom. Definitely!

Stacy was in my room. She was leaning over my bed. I stood in the doorway with my eyes nearly bugging out of my head. She had my diary in her hand. She was in the act of putting it back on my mattress and covering it with my pillow.

'Stacy!' I gasped. 'What are you doing?'

She almost jumped out of her shoes at the

sound of my voice. She spun around and stared at me. She had the weirdest expression on her face. I couldn't tell whether she looked guilty or angry or upset or just plain startled – or all four of them at once!

'Did you take my diary?' I asked.

She stared at me. She opened her mouth then closed it again without speaking.

I could feel my checks flushing. 'You *know* I never let anyone ready my diary,' I said. I felt really shocked.

'Yes,' Stacy said in a strange croaky voice. 'And now I know why.'

'I'm sorry?'

'I have to go now,' Stacy said.

I stared at her in disbelief as she shoved her things into her backpack.

'My diary is totally *personal*, Stacy,' I said as she packed up. 'I would never just take your diary and read it. Not ever.'

Stacy does keep a diary, but she only fills it in now and then, and usually only to put I HATE AMANDA in big red letters when her sister has done something exceptionally awful. My diary is different: I fill it in every single day. Stacy knows that.

She didn't say anything. She looked really angry. I couldn't really understand what was going on. I'd caught her with my diary, and yet she was acting like I'd done something to her.

'I'm going home,' she said between gritted teeth. She glared at me. 'I'm going home before I say something I shouldn't.'

'Huh? What the heck does that mean?'

Stacy glared at me. 'I really, really liked you,' she said. 'I really, really thought we'd be best friends for ever. I just hope you have a really nice time with Debbie, that's all I hope.'

'Debbie?' I screeched. 'What's Debbie got to do with anything?'

'Yeah! As if you don't know!' Stacy said. She pushed past me. 'Seeya!'

I stared after her until she disappeared out of view down the stairs, I heard the front door open and shut.

Stacy was gone. Stacy, my best friend – or maybe my ex-best friend – had stormed out of the house in a terrible mood after sneaking my personal, private, top secret diary out from under my pillow and reading it! She was gone and I was left standing there, not knowing whether to blow a fuse, scream my head off or burst into tears!

5

I ran down the stairs after Stacy. I knew I hadn't done anything wrong, but I still felt like calling out for her to come back. I wanted to know what my cousin Debbie had to do with anything. (My cousin was the only Debbie I knew, so Stacy must have meant her.) What had Stacy meant by: *I hope you have a really nice time with Debbie*?

I stopped in the hall and stared at the front door. *Hey, wait up! Why should I call her back? I hadn't done a single, solitary thing to upset her.*

I heard a patter of furtive footsteps upstairs.

I ran back up. Denny was just slipping out of my room.

'Hey, what are you up to?'

'Nuffin',' he said. That's the twins' stock answer to everything: 'Nuffin'.

He was hiding something behind his back.

'What have you got there?'

'Nuffin'.' He backed away, then made a run for his room.

'Just keep out of my room!' I yelled.

I couldn't be bothered with him and his stupid pranks right then. I went into my room and closed the door. I needed to be on my own for a little while. I needed to think.

I couldn't get my brain working. It was like everything I relied on and trusted had suddenly flipped over upside down and inside out. I sat on my bed. I opened my diary.

There was my most recent entry.

Thursday. Ms Fenwick said that Fern put the 'fern' in 'inFERNal nuisance' because she spilled glue every-where while we were making collages. The twins are still mad at me because I told Mom about the STRAWBERRY JAM. I had better watch out for revenge attacks. Arranged for Stacy to sleep over tomorrow night. Great!

I flipped back over the past few weeks, looking for an entry that Stacy might have seen and which might have made her mad at me. (Not that she should have been reading it in the first place!) There wasn't a single bad word about her. So, what was she so mad about?

I went downstairs. Dad was in the kitchen, frying eggs over-easy.

I went and stood next to him, watching as

he flipped the eggs without breaking a single yolk.

'I hope you and Stacy are hungry,' he said with a smile.

'Stacy's gone,' I said glumly.

He looked at me. 'How come? I thought I was driving the two of you to the mall later?'

I told him what had happened.

'What I can't figure out,' I finished up, 'is why *she* was mad at *me*. I didn't write anything bad about her or anything.'

'Well, maybe she was feeling guilty,' Dad said. 'You know, when people are caught doing something they know they shouldn't be doing, they sometimes react by getting angry. I bet that underneath, she was just feeling really bad about reading your diary.'

'Well, she should!' I said. 'She knows it's private. I'll never trust her again!'

Dad looked at me. 'Look, Cindy, you don't want to fall out with Stacy over this. She's your best friend, don't forget.'

'Was!' I said angrily. '*Was* my best friend.'

Dad shook his head. 'If you don't forgive her, you'll just be cutting off your nose to spite your face.'

'Huh?'

'Talk to her,' Dad said. 'Try to find out why she felt she needed to look in your diary. She

44

might have a perfectly reasonable explanation.'

'I'm not speaking to her unless she speaks to me first,' I said. 'She's in the wrong here, not me. She has to apologise.'

Dad sighed. 'That's how wars start, honey,' he said.

Yeah, well, *maybe*. But if Stacy Allen wanted to make up for what she'd done, she'd have to come to me with a really convincing apology. *Then* I might just forgive her. But otherwise, she could just go jump in the lake for all I cared!

The more I thought about it the more angry I got. I sat on the couch watching the *Galacticats* cartoon, which is all about this bunch of cats who save the Universe all the time. Yeah, like cats *do*, you know?

Then this blare of dumb music came on to announce the start of the *Splaargg the Space Mutant Show*. Two seconds later Denny and Bob came racing in and slammed themselves down on the carpet right in front of the TV. Splaargg was their big cartoon hero. Splaargg was the dumbest cartoon character ever.

I decided I was going to go up to my room and gather together everything that had anything to do with Stacy – presents from her, stuff I'd borrowed off her, et cetera. I was going to dump the whole lot in a cardboard box and throw it in the trash! That'd teach her!

But then I decided to check out the mailbox first.

There was a letter for me.

The letter. The letter I'd been waiting for, for days and days. It had finally arrived.

Remember when I told Stacy last night about the wonderful super-secret surprise that I couldn't tell her all about right then because it would spoil the wonderful super secret surprisingness of it? Well, with any luck, *this was it*.

I forgot all about dumping Stacy's stuff in a box.

I tore the envelope open.

'Yesss!'

I ran into our dining room and through into the little side room that Mom uses as her office. We call it her 'box office' because the room's so small. All you can fit in there is a computer work station, a chair and my mom. She was busy with some totally boring work stuff and had flow charts and invoice grids and miserable stuff like that up on the screen. These days Mom seems to spend most of her life working. Even when she's not *out* at work, she's nearly always tucked away in her box

46

office, tapping stuff into the computer.

Mom says it's because she has a really demanding and important job. Dad says her boss is taking advantage because she's too conscientious and doesn't know when to say *no*. Either way, Mom winds up working like crazy all the time, and it's getting so a person needs to make an appointment to see her. But I was too excited to worry about that right then. I had some big news!

'Mom! It's come!'

'That's good, honey,' she said, not even glancing my way. 'Eastern Seaboard, twenty-one thousand six hundred and eighty units.' Tappitty-tap-tap.

'It's from *My Real Best Friend!*' I said.

'Lovely,' Mom said. 'Florida and the Keys, nine thousand and twenty-one units. Hmm, not bad.' She was reading from her Filofax and typing at the same time.

I looked at her. 'Mom?'

'Yes, honey?' Tappitty-tap.

'I've killed the twins and buried them in the back yard, is that OK?'

'Sure it is, honey. No prob-' She stopped typing and looked at me. 'Excuse me? What did you say?'

I waved the letter at her. 'It's from *My Real Best Friend,*' I squealed excitedly. 'They've accepted my application to appear on the show! *I'm going to be on TV!'*

I guess I ought to explain about *My Real Best Friend*.

It's a television show. (You might have guessed that.)

Basically, it's a show on kids' TV. It's on Thursday afternoons at five o'clock. The format is really simple. The show is co-hosted by a woman called Margarita Appleyard and a guy called Max Bulmer. There are four teams on each show. The teams are made up of two people – *two best friends*. The point of the show is to find out which pair of people really are the best of friends.

The show is divided into three sections. But first of all, Margarita and Max get each team to talk a little about themselves. You know, saying stuff about how long they've known each other, and why they think they get on so well, and the nicest thing each of them has done, and all kinds of stuff like that.

Then one of the team members is put into a soundproof box for the start of the competition, while the other has to answer questions about him or her. Then the guy comes out of the soundproof box and is asked the same questions all over to see if he or she comes up with the same answers. That way you get to find out if person *one* knows as much about person *two* as they think they do.

The question can be really easy ones, like: 'What is your friend's favourite colour?' (Easy-peasy! Stacy's favourite colour is yellow.) Or they can be a little more tricky, like: 'If your friend's house was on fire, what would be the one thing she would try to save?' (Still easy in Stacy's case: she'd save her pet cat, Benjamin.)

In the next part of the show, the two teams with the highest points from the question-and-answer section have to do some complicated stuff together in a race against the clock. It's usually something like having to build a heap of weird-shaped blocks into a pyramid. The hard part being that the blocks only fit together in one order with one team member shouting instructions while the other one (blindfolded) actually has to fit the pieces together. (That's only a for instance; there are loads of different tasks.)

The winners get a whole bunch of prizes and go forward to the grand finale quick-fire quiz which could win them a vacation to Hawaii or the Swiss Alps or Disneyland or wherever.

The really great thing about the show is that it travels all around the state, so everyone gets a chance to appear in it even if they aren't able to travel very far. In a month's time, *My Real Best Friend* was going to be broadcast from Mayville – which is the very nearest town to Four Corners, where I live.

And I was going to be on the show!

I read the letter aloud to my mom.

Dear Cindy Spiegel,

I am delighted to be able to tell you that your application to be considered for *My Real Best Friend* was one of those successfully taken from the draw.

Congratulations!

As I am sure you already know, *My Real Best Friend* has proven to be one of the best-loved programmes on our network for ten- to twelve-year-olds – and YOU are now well on the way to becoming a GRAND WIN-NER!

Enclosed you will find a further application form. Please fill this in and mail or fax it back to us as soon as possible.

Remember, the family vacation of your dreams could be just a few simple questions away!

I hope to hear from you really soon.

Once your application form has been processed we will contact you with all the information you need to be part of the BEST show on TV!

Very best wishes

Valerie Sachs, Producer, *My Real Best Friend*

'That's wonderful, honey,' Mom said, giving me a hug. 'My little girl on TV! We'll have to video that, for sure! And then we'll have to make copies and send them to the whole family.'

I was just about dancing on the ceiling while I read the letter out! *Me* – on TV! Amazing! Phenomenal! Woo-hoo!

'Do you have a pen?' I asked. 'I want to fill in this form right *now*.' As you can imagine, I was pretty excited. In fact, I was just about ready to *explode*, I was so excited. I couldn't wait to tell everyone.

Mom handed me a pen and I sat on the floor by her feet.

'Write neatly, Cindy. Does it say use capitals?'

I quickly read the instructions at the top of the form. I nodded. 'Uh-huh,' I said. I filled in my name in the appropriate box: CINDY SPIEGEL.

There were a bunch of boxes for me to fill in

my address and age and birthday and telephone number and stuff like that.

Then I hit it. The BIG question.

Am I dumb or what? I'd been so excited by
the letter, and by being successful in getting on
the show that I'd forgotten something really,
really important.

Please include the following details about
the person you wish to appear with you on
My Real Best Friend.
   NAME:
   ADDRESS:
   AGE:
   DATE OF BIRTH:

I stared at the empty boxes.

Up until half an hour ago I'd been totally
certain who my real best friend was. Up until
that morning, I wouldn't have hesitated for a
single second. I'd have written: STACY
ALLEN. No problem. My all-time best friend
in all the world.

But *now*?

After what had happened that morning? Did
I really want to put Stacy down as my partner
on *My Real Best Friend* when the chances were
that we'd never speak to each other again for
the rest of our lives?

Oh heck!

Oh double heck!

Oh triple heck with golden bells on!

What a terrible time to have just split up for ever with your real best friend!

6

Mom said the bust-up between Stacy and me was just a tempest in a teapot. She said we'd make up and be best friends again in, like, twenty-four hours at most. She said she was amazed that we'd gotten this far without ever arguing. She said she argued with her best friend at school all the time. She said one of the nicest things about having a best friend is that you can have really bad fights with them and then forgive each other like nothing had happened. She said that's what best friends do.

She said I should definitely put Stacy down as my best friend for the show.

My mom is nuts!

How could I turn up on the set of *My Real Best Friend* with someone I'm never going to speak to again for the rest of my life?

Parents can be a real problem, you know? Neither my mom nor dad seemed to think that Stacy had done anything so very terrible. They treated it like she'd borrowed a pair of socks without asking. But it wasn't like that at all. My diary is utterly, utterly personal. Stacy knew that. All my friends know that. Why couldn't my mom and dad see how bad this was?

I needed to talk to my friends. Pippa and Fern would understand how I felt. They wouldn't tell me it was no big deal.

I got my dad to drive me over to the mall. Like I told you earlier, Stacy and I had arranged to meet Fern and Pippa in the main plaza under the fountain. It's not like we're total mall-rats, but we do like to go there every now and then to wander around the stores and see what's new and have lunch together. Plus we can make notes about clothes and stuff that we can go home and ask our folks to buy for us.

Not that I was in a very good position to ask for money for anything right then. My folks had bought me a clarinet. I thought a clarinet would be a real neat musical instrument to play. I mean, it just looked like an up-market recorder with its Sunday-best clothes on. But it turned out to be a total monster to play, so in the end they let me sell it on to my cousin Debbie who lives over in Hartford. But I couldn't charge her the full price, because the darned thing was second-hand by then. So I still owed my parents the balance. That was why I wasn't in a good position to bargain for any new stuff. But that didn't mean a person couldn't window-shop and make *plans*.

I found Fern sitting on the stone seat that runs right around the fountain. She was squatting there, all hunched up, with her arms folded. She was glaring straight ahead of her with an expression on her face that would have broken a bullet-proof glass mirror. I could have been wrong, but I didn't get the impression that Fern was a happy bunny right then.

'Hi,' I said. I sat down next to her.

'Hi, yourself,' Fern said.

Uh-oh. Not a good start. Fern might be the smallest of the four of us, but she makes up for it in other ways. She can be pretty loud, and she has the kind of temper that can make full-grown two-hundred-pound men dive for cover.

The weirdest thing about Fern is that she thinks she's a real peace-loving hippy-type of person. Sure, she wears way-out psychedelic weirdo clothes and listens to some really bizarre music. And she says her 'spiritual home' is San Francisco where the freaks all hang out, but, if you want my opinion of Fern, on the whole I'd day she's about as peace-loving as a hungry Tasmanian Devil with a toothache!

I hope that doesn't make it sound like I don't

like her. I do like her a whole lot, it's just that she's kind of, uh . . .*unusual*, yeah? Pippa, who is her very best friend, says that 'Fern is strange and unique'. I'll go along with that. Sometimes Fern can be as strange and unique as an alien!

'You OK?' I asked after a little while.

'I'm totally fine and dandy,' Fern said between gritted teeth.

I looked at her. 'What's wrong?'

'Nothing's wrong at all,' she growled. 'What makes you think anything is wrong?'

'Uh, maybe I think something could be wrong,' I suggested, 'because you have a face like a warthog chewing a hornet.'

Fern looked surprised. 'I do?' she said. 'Well, I'm not surprised!'

'Fern, listen, something really awful has happened,' I said. I figured that if I talked to her about Stacy, maybe that would take her mind off whatever was bugging her.

'Darn right!' Fern said.

'Huh?'

'It's the worst thing in the world when the person you thought was your very best friend turns out to be a total rat-fink!'

I stared at her. 'You *know*?' I said. 'Already?' Wow, Stacy must have been on the phone, like, ten seconds after getting home. 'What did she tell you?' I asked. If Fern had already gotten Stacy's version of events, I wanted to know what they were. And I wanted to make sure Fern knew *my* side of the story, too!

'She said I had the dress sense of a headless colour-blind parrot with terminal insanity!' Fern snarled. 'She said I ought to go hitch up with a travelling circus – if they'd have me.'

'She said *what*?' I gasped.

'She said I should carry a warning notice: bad for your eyes!' Fern growled. 'She said I should hand out free sunglasses to anyone who came within ten yards of me!'

I stared at her. Why on earth should Stacy say stuff like that to Fern? 'What did you say to her?' I asked.

'I said it was real hilarious for a person whose idea of fashion was to dress up like Morticia Addams to start bad-mouthing the clothes I wear.' She looked at me. 'I mean, let's face it, Pippa isn't exactly on the cutting edge of style, right?'

'Pippa?' I gasped. 'What's Pippa got to do with anything?'

'We're *talking* about Pippa,' Fern said.

'No we're not,' I said. 'We're talking about Stacy.'

'Stacy? *I'm* talking about Pippa!'

'It wasn't Stacy who called you?' I asked. I was getting awfully confused.

58

'Nobody called me,' said Fern. 'What the heck are you talking about, Cindy?'

I spread my hands out in front of me and took a couple of deep breaths. 'Did you or did you not get a call from Stacy this morning to tell you that we'd had a real big bust-up?'

'You had a bust-up?' Fern breathed in amazement. 'Wow. No, I didn't know that.'

'So, what were you just talking about when you said that stuff about finding out your best friend was a total rat-fink?'

'I was talking about Pippa,' Fern said. 'We just had a big bust-up.'

I stared at her in disbelief. 'You two had a bust-up, too? What *is* this?' I said. 'Bust-up Saturday, or something?'

'So, what happened with you and Stacy?' Fern asked. She shook her head. 'You won't stay mad at each other for long. No way.'

'I wish people would stop telling me that!' I said. 'I'm never going to speak to her again unless she apologises.'

'So, explain,' Fern said.

I told her the whole story.

'And if you tell me it's no big deal,' I finished off, 'I'm going to scream!'

'That's awful,' Fern said. 'I mean, it's not like I keep a diary – I think they're totally dumb – but I can see why you'd be really upset.'

59

'Well thanks!' Fern can be so tactful at times.

'And she got mad at you?' Fern said. 'I guess that was because she felt guilty at being found out.'

'That's what my dad said,' I told her.

'Maybe you should set traps?' Fern suggested. 'You know – like, keep mousetraps under your pillow, so that if anyone tried to get at your diary they'd get snapped by the trap.'

'Uh . . . I'm not sure . . . '

'Or you could coat it with one of those special anti-theft chemicals that glow under ultraviolet light,' Fern said. 'That way, you could –'

'Fern?'

'Uh-huh?'

'How come you had a fight with Pippa?' I asked. 'Do you want to tell me about it?'

'I already did,' Fern said. 'I said I needed a few new clothes to brighten myself up. And she said if I got any *brighter* they'd be able to pick me up by satellite. So I said, that's better than wandering around looking like a homesick vampire from Zombieville, Transylvania. Then she said she had taste when it came to clothes, and I said, yeah, *bad* taste!' Fern shrugged. 'And it kind of escalated from there.

I said what about that really nice, brightly coloured scarf I bought you for your birthday two years back? And she said she'd only ever worn it out of politeness and 'cos she didn't want to hurt my feelings. I said, I thought you said you lost it. And she said, I didn't lose it, I got my mom to dye it brown so I could be seen out in it! And I said, well, thanks for liking my present so much! And she said, what about the writing pack she'd bought me last Christmas that was still in its plastic wrap. And I said, sure, I'm gonna waste all my spare time writing stuff just 'cos you bought me some dumb *paper*! And she said –'

'OK! OK!' I yelled. 'I get the picture!'

Gradually, Fern calmed down. She shrugged. 'And in the end she said she never wanted to talk to me again, and she stormed off, like some total baby.'

We both sat there, staring blankly at all the people milling around the plaza.

'You know something,' Fern said after a little while. 'I think best friends are for little weenie kids. I don't think I'm going to bother having a best friend any more.' She looked at me. 'People our age should have grown out of that kind of dumb stuff by now, don't you think?'

'Uh, up to a *point*,' I said cautiously. 'I mean,

61

I sure don't want Stacy as my best friend any more.'

Fern folded her arms and leaned back. 'Yeah! No more best friends! That's the way ahead for me! No problem!'

I took the carefully folded application form for *My Real Best Friend* out of the back pocket of my jeans. I smoothed it out and handed it to Fern.

'What is it?' Fern asked.

'Take a look,' I said.

She read it slowly. 'Oh,' she said. 'Wow! I'm, like, totally stunned. Why didn't you say you'd applied for the show?'

'I didn't want to say anything in case I didn't get accepted,' I said. 'But I did.'

'Yeah. So I see,' she breathed. 'Totally brilliant!'

'The thing is,' I said, 'the only way I can get on the show is if I have a best friend to team up with me.'

'Oh, right.' Fern nodded. 'And you've just busted up with Stacy. So, I guess you won't be appearing on the show after all.'

I looked at her. 'Well, not necessarily,' I said. 'I've had an idea.'

'Yeah?'

'Yeah.' I smiled at her. 'How would *you* like to be my team-mate?'

She blinked at me a couple of times. Then she grinned. 'Really? Me?'

I smiled and nodded. 'Why not?'

She thought for a couple of seconds. 'Yeah! Why not?' she said, her eyes shining like flashlights. 'Why the heck not? We'll be great!'

Fern and I went over to the ice cream place to fill in the rest of the *My Real Best Friend* application form.

I ordered a strawberry and grape sundae and Fern had something in a tall glass called 'Chocolate Overkill'. It consisted of at least four different types of chocolate and fudge, topped off by a yard-tall swirl of cream. I could only just see Fern over it.

We perched at one of the high round tables in the foyer of the snack bar and I started filling in Fern's details on the form. You know, name, address, age.

'Your birthday's in October, right?' I said uncertainly.

Fern frowned at me from behind Chocolate Overkill mountain. 'September,' she said.

'Oh, yes. Of course,' I said with a laugh. 'Er, the twenty-something, huh?'

'Twenty-third,' Fern said.

I knew I ought to have her birthday by heart,

but I'm not very good with dates. That's why I mark out all the important dates in red ink in my diary at the start of every year. That way I don't *have* to remember.

'Yours is July, yeah?' Fern said.

'June,' I said. 'The seventeenth.'

Fern nodded. 'Yeah, that's what I meant.'

I finished filling in the form. Mom had already signed the 'parent or guardian' box at the bottom. 'That's it,' I said. 'Done, finished and complete!' I folded it and slid it into the reply-paid envelope.

We returned to our ice creams. The sealed envelope sat there on the plastic-topped table. I looked at it.

I began to feel just a little uneasy. Fern is a really good pal, and all that, but I was beginning to wonder exactly how much I really knew about her. I mean, bad as I am with dates, I could tell you Stacy's birthday without even thinking.

'Uh, Fern,' I said. 'What's your favourite colour?'

'Sky-blue pink with silver stars on,' she said with a grin. 'What about you?'

'Uh, red, I guess,' I said.

'Boring!'

I frowned at her. 'It might be boring,' I said. 'But at least a person can *remember* it. If Max

Bulmer asks me what your favourite colour is, no way am I going to be able to remember sky-blue-pink-with-silver-bells-on'.

'Silver stars,' Fern prompted.

'Exactly!'

'Look, it's a cinch,' Fern said, waving her long plastic spoon in the air. 'All we need to do is to get together a couple of times before the show and swap notes. And if either of us has problems remembering anything about the other, all we need to do is jot stuff down on little scraps of paper and hide them somewhere up our sleeves or in our socks. You know – like you do for exams.'

'I've never done that,' I said.

Fern looked at me in silence for a few moments. 'No,' she said at last. 'Neither have I. But it's the kind of thing other people do, right?'

'Fern, we'll be on TV,' I pointed out. 'Don't you think people will notice if we start pulling scraps of paper out of our socks?'

Fern thought for a while. 'I saw a movie where a guy was fed information through an electronic doodad he had stuck in his ear.' She looked at me. 'There was someone with a microphone telling him stuff, and no one knew it. Neat, huh?'

'And this helps us how, exactly?' I asked.

Fern frowned. 'Use your imagination, can't you?'

I stared at her.

She tucked cheerfully into the sludgy remains of her Chocolate Overkill.

'Sky blue pink with silver stars,' I murmured unhappily. 'Great!'

She gave me a big chocolate grin. 'You got it!' she said. 'We're gonna win by a total landslide.'

I'll say one thing for Fern, she sure has heaps of confidence.

I mailed the application form on the way home.

It felt all wrong. Even as I was putting it into the mailbox, a little voice in the back of my head was telling me this was the *wrong* thing to do. But I guess I was still too mad at Stacy to listen to sensible little voices in the back of my head.

The feeling of *wrongness* didn't get any better when I got home and Dad asked if I'd calmed down and forgiven Stacy. Well I *had* calmed down, but I sure hadn't forgiven Stacy. And even if I did forgive her (eventually – after, say, ten years), how could we ever get back to being the way we were before our big bust-up, now that I'd mailed off the *My Real Best Friend* application form with Fern's name on it?

I went up to my room for a good, long *brood*.

I could see it all! The studio. The audience. The cameras. Fern and I coming a dismal, pathetic, useless, hopeless, feeble *last place* in the competition, with the worst score in the entire history of the programme.

Max to Fern: 'What does Cindy like to drink with her breakfast?'

Fern: 'Beats me. Orange juice, maybe? Or milk? Oh, maybe pineapple and mango juice. That's what I like best. Or a chocolate milk shake? Grapefruit juice? Hey, don't sweat it, *one* of them has to be right. Yeah?'

Groan!

I began to get really mad at Stacy all over again. After all, it was her fault that I was going to be made a laughing stock on TV. If she hadn't messed with my diary, I wouldn't have had to put Fern down as my best friend. But what could I do about it? The application form was winging its way to the TV people.

I needed to think.

I thought.

I thought and thought until my brain felt completely worn out.

I still couldn't figure a way out of my dilemma.

I have a confession to make: I'm not the smartest person in the world. There, now you know. I don't mean I'm totally stupid, or anything. It's just that there are times when I have a problem and I think and think, but *nothing happens.*

Well, that's not entirely true. *Something* happens. And the something that happens is that I talk to Stacy about it. Stacy is very, very smart indeed. That's one of the reasons why she's my best friend. *Was* my best friend. But it's kind of tricky getting Stacy to help solve a problem when Stacy is the problem. Or at least, when she's a big part of the problem.

Sigh!

I decided that maybe I should talk to Mom about it. I'd just made my mind up to go down when there was this huge electronic racket from down the hall.

Bakoom! Wham! Blat! Blat! Blat! Splakowww!

I ran to the door and yelled down at the twins' room. 'Hey! Quit that noise!' Splaargg the Space Mutant was at it again. At full volume. And their bedroom door was wide open.

I guess the twins couldn't hear me over the uproar coming from the computer.

I stamped down the hall.

'Shut that thing up!' I screeched at them. I slammed their door shut real hard.

'Cindy!' It was Mom's voice from down-stairs. 'Keep it *down*! I can't hear myself think!'

I leaned over the rail. 'It's Denny and Bob,' I said.

'It's *you*,' Mom hollered. 'Stomping and crashing around like an elephant up there. I have *work* to do!'

'But –'

'I want all of you to be *quiet*!' Mom yelled. 'Is that too much to ask for five minutes?'

I didn't say anything. I could tell that Mom was getting really mad, and when my mom gets mad, saying stuff like 'It isn't my fault' doesn't really help a whole lot. In fact, it only makes things worse.

Well, so much for a quiet problem-solving talk with my mom!

There was one other option, although I was-n't all that happy about trying it out. The other option was to call Pippa and ask for her advice. If you don't know anything about Pippa, you might be wondering why I was reluctant to ask her advice. If you *do* know anything about Pippa, then you'll know *exactly* why a person would have to be desperate to turn to her. Pippa is super-intelligent and knows stuff that normal people *never* find out about. But Pippa is also a total jinx. Her advice nearly always goes haywire. Like I said, a person would have

70

to be desperate.

I was desperate.

But was I *that* desperate?

Yes, I decided. I was.

Dad was watching TV in the living room, so I called Pippa from the phone in the kitchen.

'Hi, are you OK?' I asked when she came on the line.

'No, not really,' came the morose voice down the phone. 'How 'bout you?'

'Pretty low,' I admitted.

'Yeah, I thought you would be,' Pippa said. 'Stacy called.'

'What did she say?'

'That the two of you weren't speaking,' Pippa said. 'That she didn't think she'd ever be able to speak to you again.'

'Did she say why?'

'Nope. She said it was a private thing between the two of you.' She sighed heavily down the phone. 'Do you hate her?'

'Uh, well . . . I'm not sure that I actually . . .'

'I hate Fern,' Pippa growled. 'I hate her to little tiny pieces.'

'No you don't,' I said, trying to sound up-beat. 'It was just a silly fight over nothing. You'll be friends with her again in no time, I bet you will.' (I was beginning to sound like *Mom*! Weird!)

71

'No way,' Pippa said firmly. 'I'm never going to speak to her again. She's totally horrible.' She paused for breath. 'Anyway, what actually happened with you and Stacy?'

I told her.

Then I told her that I had been invited to appear on *My Real Best Friend*.

'Ee-oo-wooooooooh!' Pippa exclaimed. 'Ee-ooh-ahhh-oooh-woooh! That's super-mega-amazing, Cindy! That's brilliant!'

'Well, yeah, but –'

'That's incredible! Gee, that's so fabulous, Cindy! Wow! Wow-wow-wow-wow!' She made a noise like a tea kettle coming to the boil. 'Wheeeeeeeeeezooop!'

'Yes, but –'

'You gotta make up with Stacy,' Pippa blurted. 'You've got to make up with her right *now*! This *second*!'

'It's too late!' I howled down the phone. 'I've already sent the application form back with Fern's name on it. It's too late!'

Silence.

'Pippa?'

'Oh, heck! If you want my opinion, I'd say that's a pretty disastrous thing to have done, Cindy,' she said, helpfully.

'I agree,' I said.

'Uh . . . what are you going to do?' Pippa

asked. 'I mean, Stacy will be really upset at being snubbed like that.'

'Well, if we're never going to speak to each other again, I guess a little thing like blowing her out of an appearance on TV won't make much difference,' I said, trying to make it sound less awful than it really was. I felt tears pricking at the back of my eyes. I bit my lip to stop myself bursting out crying. This was supposed to be the best day of my life. It had turned into a total nightmare!

'I guess not,' Pippa said.

I dabbed at my eyes and snuffled a little. I felt really wretched.

'So, uh, what's the plan?' Pippa asked.

'I don't know,' I wailed. 'Oh, rats! Hold on!' I put the phone down and went to reel off a few sheets of kitchen towel. I guess it had finally hit me how awful all this really was. I just hoped no one came into the kitchen and found me howling my eyes out like that. The twins would have a ball!

'Are you OK?' Pippa asked.

'Yush,' I snuffled.

'You don't *sound* OK,' Pippa said.

'All right!' I wailed. 'I'm not OK. I'm not OK at all. I'm totally un-OK!'

'I thought so,' said Pippa. 'Don't cry, Cindy. You'll start me off.'

I put a lot of effort into getting a grip. The last thing I needed was for Pippa to start sobbing down the phone at me.

'I'm fine now,' I said. The tears had stopped and I was back in control – just!

'*Schnuuuunf*!' went Pippa down the phone.

'Pippa? Are you crying?'

'I'm sorry,' Pippa wailed. 'I can't help it. Fern was so awful to me, Cindy. Do you know what she said? She said I dressed like . . .' I couldn't quite make out what she said next because she broke down in tears. It sounded a little like 'Mortishhyahhyahhhyummmms.'

'She was angry,' I said. 'People say things they don't mean when they're angry. You know how much Fern likes you, really.'

'I don't think she does,' Pippa moaned. 'Not any more.'

'Of course she does!' I said. Heck! How had this happened? I'd called Pippa for some tender loving care, and all of a sudden I was sitting there trying to make her feel better.

'Nope,' Pippa snuffled. 'We're never going to talk to each other again. I don't even want to *see* her again. If I ever see her again I'm going to totally ignore her. I hate her.'

'Look,' I said. 'What say we get together tomorrow? Just the two of us?'

'Yeah, right!' Pippa said, starting to sound a

little more cheerful. 'We don't need them.' She gave a long sniff. 'We can have a great time without Stacy *or* Fern!'

'Too right!' I said. 'We don't need either of them!'

I hope that I sounded more convinced than I felt.

Still, I managed to get back to my room before the next wave of misery hit me.

What an awful day!

I hardly slept at all that night. At two o'clock in the morning, I was feeling so miserable that I very nearly got up and called Stacy to tell her I didn't care about the diary. I wanted us to be friends again!

And then I thought what she would say when she found out I had invited Fern to be my partner on *My Real Best Friend*.

Things Stacy Might Say On Being Told That Fern Was Going to Be My Partner On My Real Best Friend*:*

1. Wow! That's exciting! I'm really pleased for you, Cindy, and I'm not in the tiniest bit jealous.

2. Excuse me? FERN? Since when has Fern been your best pal? I'm your best pal! How could you do this to me?

3. You are a total rat-fink-skunk-toad-swamp-monster-from-the-pits and I will hate you for the rest of your life – if you live that long!

Option three seemed most likely, in the circumstances.

I decided not to call Stacy after all.

I finally got to sleep only to be woken up, like, ten minutes later by the twins. They were hurtling around the house at the crack of dawn. I crammed the pillow down over my head. The last thing I heard was my dad, yelling.

'Denny! Bob! Do you know what time it is? I don't want to hear a peep out of either of you for the next two hours!'

Ahh! Thanks, Dad.

Later on that morning I took out my bike and cycled on over to Pippa's place. It's strange, but I didn't feel anything like so bad as I had during the night. Why do things seem more awful at two o'clock in the morning than they do at ten o'clock in the morning? I'd have to ask Stacy. She knows strange stuff like that. Darn it! I *couldn't* ask Stacy.

Hey, but I could ask Pippa. Granted, I might not understand her answer. Half the time I can't understand a word she says! I mean, what's the use in being a total brainbox if no one can figure out a thing you're saying?

That was the great thing about Stacy. We

really understood each other, you know? It was like –

Arrgh! I must shut up about Stacy!

I decided I was going to be really sympathetic towards Pippa. I figured that if I was busy sympathising with her about her bust-up with Fern, then I might forget for a little while how bad I was feeling about Stacy.

It's called 'occupational therapy'.

Mrs Kane was out in the drive, dressed in overalls and doing something greasy and oily under the hood of their car. Pippa's mom is really practical with stuff like that. I'll tell you one thing: she sure didn't pass her practicalness on to her daughter! Pippa has problems switching on a *light*.

'Hi, Cindy,' Mrs Kane said, smiling greasily at me.

'Hi, is Pippa around?'

'Sure. Go in.'

I went into their house. The first thing people notice about Pippa's house is that it's full of books. Pippa's mom is a college lecturer. Mega-brainy.

I went straight upstairs. It was kind of comforting to me that with all her brains, Pippa was no better off than I was when it came to bust-ups with her friends. I walked along the landing to Pippa's room. Poor Pippa. I was going to comfort her in her hour of need. And maybe she could comfort me, too, in my hour of need. I was never going to talk to Stacy again, and Pippa was never going to talk to . . .

'Fern!' I stared into Pippa's room with my eyes out on stalks.

'Hi,' Fern said cheerfully. She was sitting cross-legged on Pippa's bed, large as life and twice as colourful.

'Hello, Cindy,' Pippa said in a squashed kind of voice. 'Just a second.' She was upside down. She was doing a head-stand in the middle of the floor. Her long, skinny legs wobbled and she came tumbling down on to cushions. 'Ooch! Phoo!' She sat up, her face beet red. 'How'd I do?' she asked Fern.

'Three minutes and five seconds,' Fern said.

'Excellent!' She grinned at me. 'I read on the Internet that if you stand on your head for five minutes every day, the increased blood flow to your brain will make you up to seventeen per cent smarter.' She picked up a notebook and scribbled in it. 'So,' she said. 'I only have to stand on my head for one minute and fifty-five seconds more today, and I'll be on target.'

I was speechless. The upside-down stuff was weird enough, but the thing I couldn't get over was that Fern and Pippa were in there together like nothing had ever happened.

'Would it work the same if you stood on your head once a week for thirty-five minutes?' Fern asked.

'I don't know about that,' Pippa said thoughtfully. 'I guess a person can have too much blood going to their brain all at once.'

'Yeah,' Fern chuckled. 'Your head might explode!'

'What's going on?' I finally managed to ask.

'I told you,' Pippa said. 'I'm working to increase my mental powers by –'

'No! No! No!' I said. 'I'm not talking about *that*.' I pointed to Fern. 'You're here.'

Fern blinked at me. 'I guess I am,' she said.

'But . . . but you shouldn't be. The two of you had a terrible argument. You were never going to speak to each other again for the rest of your lives, no way, never, ever. You *said*.'

'Oh, that was yesterday.' Fern waved a dismissive hand at me. 'We're OK now.'

'But –'

'We were both upset and overwrought,' Pippa said. (Over-*what*?) 'We had a clash of bad bio-rhythm days, that's all,' she said. 'I checked it out on a bio-rhythm site on the Internet. Yesterday we were both in emotional, mental and physical troughs.' She grinned at Fern. 'Of course, as soon as I found out, I called Fern and we patched things up.'

'Yeah,' Fern agreed cheerfully. 'Bio-rhythms can be a real drag.' She smiled at me. 'But we're both on the up today.'

'Bio-rhythms?' I mumbled. 'Bad . . . bio . . . rhyth . . . ums. . . ?' I felt a little dazed.

Fern and Pippa getting back together had kind of pulled the rug out from under me.

'Yes,' Pippa said. 'Maybe you should check yours out.'

'Fine,' I said. 'Whatever you say.'

We went into the room where they kept their computer and looked up my bio-rhythms. Emotional low. Physical high. Mental in-between. Nothing much to go on there. Then we looked up Stacy's bio-rhythms. She was on a mental and physical high but in an emotional trough.

'There's your answer,' Pippa said authoritatively. 'You're both experiencing emotional low points.'

'Meaning what, exactly?' I asked.

'Meaning you should call her and explain that she only did what she did because she was in an emotional trough,' Pippa said. 'Tell her you understand and that you forgive her.'

'I see,' I said slowly. 'And she'll go for that, do you think?'

'Sure, she will,' Fern said. 'And then you can tell her all about appearing on *My Real*

Best Friend. She'll get a real kick out of that, I bet.'

I looked at them. 'You don't think she'll be mad that I didn't pick her as my partner?'

Fern smiled at me. 'I sure would be,' she said happily. 'I'd break every bone in your body!' She saw the alarmed look on my face. 'But that's only *me*,' she said hastily. 'Stacy wouldn't act like that. Stacy'll understand. Trust me.'

'Fern's right,' Pippa said, nodding encouragingly. 'Call Stacy. Call her right now.' She picked up the phone and handed it to me.

'I don't know . . .' I said.

Fern tapped out Stacy's number. 'Go for it!' she said. 'What have you got to lose?'

I held the phone to my ear. It was ringing. What did I have to lose? Every bone in my body, that's what!

9

Someone at Stacy's end picked the phone up.

'Hello?' said a voice I could only just hear over a loud roaring, churning noise. I was pretty sure it was Stacy.

'Hello?' I said.

'What? I can't hear you.'

'I said, hello,' I yelled.

'Oh! It's you! Hi!' she yelled.

'Uh . . . what's that noise?' I asked.

'Huh?'

'The noise!' I hollered. Pippa and Fern looked at me like I was nuts.

'Oh. Nothing. It's only my idiot sister vacuuming the idiot hall carpet. Hold on a minute.' I heard a muffled yell of: 'Give me a break! Turn that darned thing off!'

I looked at Fern and Pippa. 'Someone's vacuuming the carpets over there,' I explained.

The 'darned thing' wasn't turned off. In fact it got louder. 'My sister is so inconsiderate,' she muttered down the phone. 'Hey!' she asked me. 'When are you coming over?'

'You *want* me to come over?' I said.

'Huh? You'll have to speak up,' she hollered. 'I can't hear you.'

'I said,' I yelled, 'I didn't think you'd want me to come over.'

'Why not?' she hollered back.

'Because of *that stuff*,' I shrieked. 'You know – yesterday morning.'

'What about yesterday morning?' she bellowed over the noise of the vacuum, which was getting louder by the second.

'My *diary*!' I howled. 'Look, I feel really bad about all this. I really want us to be friends again. Can we be –' The noise of the vacuum cleaner cut out. 'FRIENDS AGAIN!'

'Ow! Yeowch! Quit hollering, Natalie. You wanna bust my eardrums, or what?'

Now that the noise of the vacuum was gone, I had the feeling I wasn't talking to Stacy at all. 'Who is that?' I asked.

'Who's *that*?' she said.

'Cindy.'

'Huh?'

'Cindy Spiegel.'

'You dumb idiot! What's the idea of calling me up and pretending to be Natalie?' It was Stacy's airhead sister, Amanda.

84

'I was not pretending to be Natalie!' I said, really offended. Natalie Smith has an awful, shrieky, squeaky voice. She sounds like a gopher on helium. Come to that, she *looks* like a gopher on helium, too! 'And I didn't call you up, I called Stacy up.'

'So, why didn't you say so?' Amanda said. 'Are you some kind of total idiot or something?'

I wasn't really in the mood for an argument with Stacy's half-wit sister. 'Could I speak to Stacy, please,' I said, really politely. 'Thank you,' I added for good measure.

'Hey, small fry,' I heard Amanda call. 'It's one of your dumb buddies.'

'Who?' I could just hear Stacy's voice in the distance.

'Cindy.'

'I don't want to speak to her,' I heard Stacy say.

'So, tell her,' Amanda said.

I heard Stacy say, 'You tell her!'

'Tell her what?'

'Tell her I'm not home,' Stacy said.

'Hello? Cindy?' Amanda said into the phone. 'Stacy says to tell you she doesn't want to speak to you and she's not home, OK?'

I felt all churned up inside again with annoyance and hurt. 'Well, you can just tell her that

I don't want to speak to her, then,' I hollered down the phone, hoping Stacy would be able to hear me. 'And you can tell her I'm not home either! So there!' I slammed the phone down.

'Hey,' Fern said, looking at me. 'There's steam coming out of your ears!'

'How'd it go?' Pippa asked.

'Don't ask!' I said. 'She wouldn't even talk to me. But that's just fine, 'cos I don't want to talk to her.' I glared at them. 'You should never have gotten me to make that call. I knew it wouldn't work! Stacy's the most stubborn, awkward person in the whole world.' I shook myself angrily. 'Well, that's it! I'm through trying to be nice to her. She's had it as far as I'm concerned. She can just go down into her back yard and eat worms for all I care!'

'So,' Pippa said cautiously. 'It didn't go too well, then?'

'Hey, look on the bright side,' Fern said. 'You still have us!'

'What we need to ascertain,' Pippa said, 'is the kind of information the two of you will need to possess about one another if you are going to achieve your full potential on *My Real Best Friend*.'

Pippa was sitting cross-legged on her desk. She reminded me of the caterpillar in *Alice in*

Wonderland. She was making about as much sense! I was sitting on the floor and Fern was sprawled out on the bed.

Fern lifted an arm "Scuse me,' she said. 'You want to go over that again in *English*?'

Pippa frowned at her. 'You need to figure out the kind of questions they're going to ask you on the TV show,' Pippa said with a sigh.

'Should we make a list of all the kinds of questions they ask?' I suggested.

'Good idea!' Pippa said. She took out a notepad. 'OK. First question. Uh . . . I know! Favourite colour!'

'Easy!' I said. 'Fern's favourite colour is sky-blue pink with silver stars on!'

'Wrong!' Fern said.

I stared at her. 'But you told me –'

'That was yesterday,' Fern said airily. 'Today my favourite colour is burnt orange and mauve with electric-blue zigzags.' She blinked at me. 'I have a different favourite colour every day.'

'Arrgh!' I said. 'She's nuts! We're doomed!'

'What's the problem?' Fern said.

'Hold up!' Pippa said. 'Burnt orange and mauve with electric-blue zigzags isn't a colour!'

'Sure it's a colour,' Fern said. 'What the heck else is it?'

'I mean it isn't *a* colour,' Pippa explained. 'It's three different colours. If someone asks you what your favourite colour is, you can't tell them three different colours.'

'Why not?' Fern asked.

'You just *can't*!' Pippa snorted. 'It's against the rules.'

'Well, that's just dumb,' Fern said.

'Stacy likes yellow best,' I moaned to myself.

'And you like red best,' Fern said to me. 'See? I remember.' She looked carefully at me. 'Do you still like red best?'

'Yes. Of course.'

'Favourite food!' Pippa interrupted, trying to get the conversation back on line. 'Cindy, what do you like best to eat?'

'Strawberry ice cream,' I said. 'Oh. Or my mom's home-made chilli.'

'Got it, Fern said. 'Chilli and strawberry ice cream.'

'Don't say it like that. Not both together like that,' I said. 'You'll make me sound like a crazy person. Anyway, what's your favourite food?' I asked a little reluctantly. I was kind of dreading the answer. Knowing Fern it could be steak and custard with an anchovy garnish!

'Grilled cheese,' she said. Hooray! A nice, simple, straightforward answer for once. 'Cheese on toast, *à la* Kipsak!' she continued.

She raised a hand. 'Listen and learn,' she said. 'Take one slice of lightly toasted bread. Spread with butter and a thick layer of barbecue sauce. Next, add a slice of ham and splurge all over with mustard. Slice some cheese and lay a thin layer over this. Then chop up an onion and spread the pieces on top of the cheese. Mix equal portions of ketchup and mayonnaise to a pink paste. Blob this on to the onion and then add a second layer of cheese. Finally, sprinkle a tiny amount of cayenne pepper on top, and pop into the oven for five minutes. There you go. Cheese on toast *à la* Kipsak!' She beamed at us. 'It's my own recipe, you know.'

'Really?' I said with a big dose of irony. 'I find that hard to believe!'

'I'll make it for us next time you come around to my place,' Fern said.

'Yeah, right,' Pippa said 'Make sure you have the medics on standby!'

'It's great, honest,' Fern protested. 'You've never tasted anything like it – guaranteed!'

'I can believe it!' I said.

'Can we get back to the point?' Pippa asked. 'Favourite pop group.'

'Jefferson Airplane!' Fern said. 'Mega-fan-tastic!'

'Who?' I asked. 'I've never even *heard* of them.'

'No one's even heard of them,' Pippa added. 'She's just being a pain. Come on, Fern. Pick a group people will know.'

'Oh, OK, Walking on Air, I guess,' Fern said. 'Their last single was pretty neat and Cal Hooper's kind of cute.'

'Cute like a land-fill site,' I said. 'He's a total slob.'

'Excuse me!' Pippa bellowed. 'Can we get back to the point, please, guys? You don't have to agree on stuff. You just need to know what each of you likes best. We have to get the two of you up to speed about each other so that you have at least a halfway decent chance of looking like you know each other when you appear on *My Real Best Friend*!'

She was right, of course.

'Hey!' Fern said suddenly. 'I'd forgotten about French Toast! Their last song was totally brilliant.' She looked at Pippa. 'Yeah, cross our Walking on Air and put me down for French Toast instead.'

'I can't cope with this!' I hollered. 'She changes her mind every five minutes! She's totally out of her mind!'

Fern looked at me in surprise. 'I get bored easy,' she said with a shrug.

I put my head in my hands.

'OK, OK,' Pippa said, waving her arms for

attention. 'I think I have a solution to this.' She looked at Fern. 'I agree with Cindy: you're a nut!'

'Hey!' Fern said. 'Do you mind!'

'Listen! It doesn't matter.' She pointed at me. '*You* go in the soundproof box and Fern answers questions about you, right? That way it doesn't matter if Fern likes puce-with-amber-stripes one minute and fluorescent-green-with-yellow-polkadots-and-pink-splats the next.'

'Yeah, that doesn't sound so bad,' I said. I looked at Fern. 'Do you remember what colour I like best?'

'Sure. Red,' Fern said. 'And your favourite food is chilli and ice cream, but not at the same time.'

'Good,' Pippa said. 'That's a great start.' She looked seriously at us. 'And now, Fern, you're gonna learn more about Cindy than you ever thought possible.'

Pippa looked really determined. I crossed my fingers. I really hoped this was going to work.

After maybe half an hour of Pippa firing questions at me, and Fern repeating everything I said, we tried the big test. I was sent out of the room while Pippa asked Fern a series of questions about me. If she'd been paying attention, she should know all the answers. And if she knew all the answers, we at least had a chance!

I sat on the stairs. Mrs Kane had finished working on the car and the front door was shut. All around me, the landing was lined with bookshelves filled with books. Jeepers, that was a booky house! Even their cellar was filled with boxes of books. A person could go blind just *thinking* about all those words!

I picked a book off one of the shelves, just to see what kind of stuff Pippa and her mom liked to read.

'*Communication Studies*,' I read. '*The art and science of human communication.*' I opened it. OK, so far so good. I read the first sentence. 'A meta-communicational axiom of the pragmatics of communication can be postulated: it is impossible to not communicate.'

My brain did a backward somersault. I quickly put the book back. Pippa and her mom were totally insane!

The doorbell rang.

I waited for Mrs Kane to come and answer it.

It rang a second time.

'Hey, could someone get the door for me?' I heard Mrs Kane call from the back of the house. 'I'm on the telephone!'

I trotted down the stairs, walked along the hallway and opened the door.

'Oh!' I said.

'Oh!' Stacy said back.

I stood there, staring at her and kind of wishing the floor would open up and swallow me.

It didn't.

'Hello,' Stacy said stiffly. 'I didn't know you'd be here.'

I blinked at her. Why hadn't the floor opened up like I wanted it to?

'Yes, well,' I said just as stiffly back. 'I am.'

'So I see,' Stacy said.

'Uh . . . yes,' I said.

'Uh . . . well,' Stacy said.

What next? Read any good books lately? Nice weather for the time of year? Do you come here often?

'Did you want Pippa?' I asked with a polite little smile.

'When I come to Pippa's house,' Stacy said, 'it's usually because I want Pippa.' She smiled back. It was about as friendly as a smile as you might see on the face of a piranha just before it attacks you.

I stepped aside. 'She's in her room,' I said.

'Thank you,' Stacy said, coming into the house.

'You're welcome,' I said.

Stacy marched upstairs. I trailed after her. Talk about embarrassing!

Pippa was standing at the top of the stairs. 'Hi, Stacy,' she said. 'C'mon up. We're just rehearsing for . . . ahh! Um, oh . . . you know . . . er . . .' Pippa had realised mid-sentence that maybe that wasn't the best way of introducing Stacy to the idea of Fern and me appearing together on *My Real Best Friend*.

'Rehearsing for what?' Stacy asked.

'Oh nothing,' Pippa mumbled. 'Nothing in particular. Ha, ha. Just . . . *life* . . . . you know? Ulp! Hey, that's a nice T-shirt, Stacy. Is it new?'

'It was six months ago,' Stacy said, sounding puzzled.

We all went into Pippa's room.

'Yo, Stacy!' Fern said with a big smile. 'Are you and Cindy pals again or are you still acting like a couple of prize-winning nerds?'

'No, we are not friends again,' Stacy said very crisply. 'And if anyone's behaving like a prize-winning nerd, it sure isn't me.'

I looked at Pippa. 'I hope Stacy isn't suggesting that I'm acting like a prize-winning nerd,' I said. 'Because anyone who thinks I'm a prize-winning nerd, is a total rat-fink, in my opinion.'

'So,' Fern said, looking at Stacy, 'I guess you won't be in the audience cheering us on when we break all the records on *My Real Best Friend*.'

Stacy looked confused. 'You guess I won't be doing what when you do which?'

'Oh, didn't anyone tell you?' Fern said, ploughing on like a blindfolded cow in a porcelain store. 'Cindy and I are appearing on *My Real Best Friend* when it comes to Mayville. Isn't that something else?' She laughed. 'Pippa's been rehearsing us for the question and answer section.'

Pippa and I glared at Fern. If there *was* a good way to tell Stacy about this stuff, Fern had definitely missed it by a million miles.

Fern blinked at us. 'What?' she said. 'What'd I say now?'

'Oh, nothing,' Pippa sighed.

I was thinking of a phrase that had the words 'big' and 'mouth' in it!

I gave Stacy a sidelong glance. She was just standing there, staring at Fern with a blank look on her face. Then she turned her head and looked straight at me.

Argh! If looks could kill, my folks would have been picking flowers for my grave.

'How very nice for the two of you,' Stacy said icily. 'How did you come to be picked for the show, then?'

'Oh, you know,' I stumbled on. 'It was . . . like . . . um . . .'

'Cindy sent off an application,' Fern said cheerfully. 'She was going to put you down as her best friend, but since the two of you aren't speaking, she put me down instead.'

'I see,' Stacy said. She gave me a ferocious look. I hope the two of you do really well. I'm sure you know tons of stuff about each other.'

'I'm not so sure they do,' Pippa said. 'That's the problem. Fern is hopeless at remembering stuff – '

'Hey! Do you mind?' Fern interrupted.

'What's Cindy's favourite vacation destination?' Pippa asked her.

'Uh . . . Disneyland!' Fern said.

'Universal Studios!' I yelled. 'I just told you ten minutes ago!'

'Yeah, yeah, keep your hair on,' Fern said. 'I meant Universal Studios. It was a slip of the tongue.'

'See the problem?' Pippa said to Stacy.

Stacy smirked. 'Yes,' she said. 'Yes, I do. It sure doesn't look like the two of you will be jetting off to any dream vacations in the near future.' I guess she was really enjoying the fact that Fern and I were about as well-matched to appear together on *My Real Best Friend* as a humpbacked whale and a chipmunk playing on a see-saw!

'Maybe you could help me coach them?' Pippa said to Stacy. She consulted her notepad. 'Look, here's a question: what would your best friend do if she won half a million dollars in the lottery?' Pippa looked at me. 'Go on, Cindy. Try it out. What would Fern do?'

I thought carefully. 'She'd go and live in San Francisco,' I said. 'In a beach house.' I guessed that was probably pretty near the mark: Fern was always saying how San Francisco was her 'spiritual home' – whatever that meant!

'Nope,' Fern said. 'Totally wrong,'

'She'd build an observatory,' Pippa said. She looked at Fern. 'Wouldn't you?'

'Got it in one!' Fern said with a grin. 'So I can keep an eye on all those darned aliens out there!'

Rats! I'd forgotten. Fern's other big obsession is with aliens. She has a theory that aliens are gradually taking over the world by impersonating earth-people. Jeepers! And this was the person I was appearing on TV with? Help!

'OK, strike one,' Pippa said. 'Fern? What would Cindy do with half a million dollars?'

Fern looked thoughtfully at me. She scratched her head. She chewed her lips. She frowned. She scratched her head again. Time passed. She gazed out of the window. Her eyes glazed over.

'Fern?' Pippa asked.

'Huh? Oh, sorry,' Fern said. 'I was just thinking about owning my own observatory. That would be so cool! What was the question again?'

'What would Cindy do!' Pippa raved. 'Lottery winnings! Half a million dollars!'

'Oh, yeah.' Fern looked at me again. 'I dunno,' she said. 'She'd . . .uh . . . she'd have a diamond stud put in her nose.'

'I'd *what*?' I screeched. 'Are you out of your mind? I don't want a diamond stud in my nose!'

'She'd probably use it to move on over to Hartford to be closer to her cousin Debbie,' Stacy said coldly. 'And to be further away from people she pretends to like but doesn't really.'

I stared at her.

She stared right back.

'Will you ask Stacy what the heck my cousin Debbie has got to do with anything?' I asked Pippa. This was the second time Stacy had referred to Debbie, and I was still no closer to figuring out how Debbie fitted into the picture. Debbie lived miles away. I hadn't even seen Debbie for six months. I was beginning to think Stacy had some kind of weird Debbie-fixation that had warped her mind.

'Tell her she already *knows* what her cousin Debbie has to do with it,' Stacy said to Pippa. 'She knows darned well!'

'I do not know darned well at all!' I yelled.

'Do, too!'

'Don't!'

'OK!' Pippa yelled. She lifted her arms in the air. 'How about a cease-fire, guys, before someone gets mown down in the cross-fire!'

'She started it,' I muttered.

'Did not!' Stacy growled.

'Did too!' I snarled. 'You sneaked my diary out from under my pillow!'

Stacy turned angrily to face me, her fists on her hips. 'That's not true! I was putting it *back*!' She glared daggers at me. 'And if a person is going to write a nasty letter about another person, then that person should be a darned sight more careful about where they *put* that letter!'

'OK, guys!' Pippa hollered at the top of her voice. 'Gang meet!'

Our gang doesn't have a whole lot of rules, but one rule we do have is that if any one of us yells 'Gang meet!' then we all have to stop whatever we're doing and get together for a pow-wow.

With Stacy and me not speaking to one another (sure, we were yelling, but we weren't *speaking*), I wasn't at all sure we still *had* a gang. But rules are rules, so both of us shut up and turned to look at Pippa.

'Excuse me if I'm wrong,' Pippa said sternly, frowning from me to Stacy, 'but it sounds to me like the two of you need to sit down and actually *listen* to one another for a minute or two!' She gave us one of her I'm-in-charge looks. 'I propose we convene a court of sessions to consider the question of who did what to whom.' She patted her chest. 'And I'm judge!'

'Yeah, but –' I started.

'No, but –' Stacy said at the same time.

Fern whacked her hand against the wall. 'Silence in court!' she said. 'Judge Pippa presiding!'

'Thank you, Fern,' Pippa said. She climbed up on to her desk and sat there with her arms folded. 'Now then,' she said. 'The plaintiffs will be given the opportunity to put their cases to the court one at a time.'

'Yo! Tell it like it is, Pippa!' Fern said.

'Silence, or I shall have the court cleared,' Pippa said, frowning at Fern. 'Now, Cindy. What is your beef with Stacy?'

'Why should –' Stacy began.

Judge Pippa raised her hand to shut Stacy up. 'You'll have your turn in a minute,' Pippa said. 'Cindy gets to speak first.'

I gave Stacy a triumphant smirk. She stuck her tongue out at me. She can be so childish at times! I stuck my tongue out at her and went cross-eyed. Hah! That showed her!

'I caught Stacy red-handed with my secret diary,' I told Pippa. I pointed at Stacy. 'Just let her try and deny it! Just let her try!'

Pippa looked at Stacy. 'Well?'

'I found Cindy's diary on the floor when I was folding up the inflatable mattress,' Stacy said. 'I was putting it back when she walked into the room.'

I stared at her. 'So, why didn't you say so?' I said. I looked at Pippa. 'Get her to answer that,' I said. 'Why didn't she say so at the time?'

'Because I saw the *letter*!' Stacy stormed.

'What letter?' I yelled.

'The letter you'd written to your cousin Debbie!' Stacy said.

'Are you out of your mind?' I yelled at her. 'I never wrote any letter to my cousin Debbie!' I looked at Pippa. 'I submit, your honour, that Stacy is making stuff up to try to disguise her crime!' (Hey, I thought, way to go, Cindy! That was as good as a court-room drama on

102

TV!)

'It was folded up in the pages of the diary,' Stacy hollered at Pippa. 'It fell out when I picked the diary up. It was a letter from Cindy to her cousin Debbie – and it said some awful things about me in it!'

'There wasn't any letter!' I howled. 'This is ridiculous!'

Fern banged the wall again. 'Silence in court!' she shouted. 'The next person to yell gets thrown out!'

'Quit yelling!' Pippa told her.

'I'm not yelling,' Fern yelled. 'Stacy and Cindy are doing the yelling!'

'We are not!' I yelled.

'Shut up!' Pippa howled.

Everyone shut up.

'Good!' Pippa said. 'That's more like it. I think we could use a little more decorum in here, OK, guys?'

'Huh?' Fern said.

'Cool it!' Pippa explained. She looked at Stacy. 'You say there was a letter tucked into Cindy's diary.'

'I sure do,' Stacy said. 'A letter from Cindy to her cousin Debbie. And it said totally horrible things about me! Really hurtful *personal* things. About how she only *pretends* to be my friend. And that I *smell*.'

'Not true!' I said. 'I never wrote a letter like that.' I looked at Stacy. 'Why would I say that about you?' I said. 'You don't smell bad.'

Stacy blinked at me 'But . . . but . . .'

'Did you recognise Cindy's writing on the alleged letter?' Judge Pippa asked.

Stacy looked at her. 'Well, no. It was a print-out. I figured Cindy had written it on her computer.'

I shook my head. 'It wasn't me,' I said. 'Honest. Did it *say* it was from me?'

'Yes,' Stacy said uncertainly. 'At the bottom of the letter it said: "from Cindy."'

'Was there a signature?' Judge Pippa asked.

'Well . . . no-o-o . . .' Stacy admitted.

'I don't put *from* Cindy, at the bottom of letters. I put *love*, Cindy.'

Stacy stared at me. 'It wasn't from you?'

'No!' I said. 'It darned well wasn't!'

'A forgery!' Judge Pippa exclaimed. 'An evil, fiendish forgery!'

'But who the heck would want to . . .' My voice trailed off. Certain things suddenly clicked in my mind. It had been the twins' turn to use our home computer on Friday. They had it in their room playing their dumb Space Mutant games on it! What was to stop them making up a nasty letter? A nasty letter in which I bad-mouthed Stacy to my cousin

104

Debbie!

Stacy and I looked at each other. 'Denny and Bob!' we both yelled together.

Denny and Bob! My horrible, horrible little brothers! They'd set the whole thing up to cause trouble between Stacy and me!

Graaahrrrrr!

Death to Denny and Bob!

11

'Cindy, I'm so sorry!' Stacy gasped. 'The letter
. . . I . . . it . . . I thought you *hated* me!'

'And I thought you *hated* me!' I said. 'But I
couldn't figure why!'

'I never hated you!' Stacy said. 'You're my
best friend!'

I grinned. Phee-ew! Talk about a total *relief*!
I felt like a whole mountain had just lifted off
my back. 'It's mutual!' I said, really meaning it.
I gave her an anxious look. 'I'm very sorry that
you're not going to be my team-mate for *My
Real Best Friend*. I *wanted* to put your name
down, but I didn't think we were ever going to
speak to each other again. And now I've ruined
it and you won't be on TV with me and I won't
win a *thing*!'

'Excuse me,' Fern chipped in. 'Second
choice TV partner within earshot!'

'Sorry, Fern,' I said. 'I don't mean you're
useless, or anything. I just don't think we're
completely compatible, that's all. Not like

Stacy and me.'

'Quitter!' Fern said with grin. 'But apology accepted.'

Stacy smiled at me. 'It doesn't matter about the TV show,' she said bravely. 'I don't care about stuff like that.' She paused and thought for a moment. 'Well, I do care about it, but not as much as I care about us being friends again! That's what really matters.'

'Yes!' I said. 'And in future, if we ever have an argument, we'll sit down and not leave the room until we've talked it through like proper grown-up adult people.'

'Don't worry,' Stacy said with a huge grin. 'We'll never argue again. Guaranteed!'

Stacy is a really great person. And she was right, if I had anything to do with it, we'd never fall out again! Ever!

'Is this court still in session, or what?' Fern asked.

'It is,' Judge Pippa said. 'I think we have enough evidence now to make a ruling.'

Judge Pippa scribbled furiously in her notepad for a while.

'OK, guys,' she said. 'Here are the findings of the Four Corners supreme court case of Stacy versus Cindy. We find that the whole thing was a misunderstanding, possibly caused by a fiendish and evil plot by Cindy's rotten little brothers, Bob and Denny.'

'Possibly!' I yelled. 'You've got to be kidding! They *did* it! Definitely!'

'There's only circumstantial evidence that they were involved,' Judge Pippa pointed out.

'Give me a break!' I said. 'How much evidence do you need?'

'Hey,' Judge Pippa looked sternly at me. 'In *my* court, everyone is innocent until proven guilty!'

'I'll get proof,' I said between gritted teeth. 'And then I'll slaughter 'em!'

I *knew* what they had done, as clear as if I could *see* it.

They'd made up a letter on the computer that bad-mouthed Stacy and seemed to have been written by me. (They had to do it on the computer or Stacy would have seen right away that it wasn't my handwriting!) Then they took my diary out from under my pillow on Saturday morning while I was downstairs. They put the letter in the pages of the diary so it stuck right out, and put the diary somewhere where Stacy couldn't miss it. They folded the letter with the typing outside, so Stacy couldn't help but see the way the letter was headed. (Stacy filled me in on this. The heading, in big, bold, black lettering, was: **Ways In Which**

Stacy Allen Stinks! Kind of eye-catching, huh?)

Stacy thought my diary had slid out from under my pillow. She was just going to put it back when she saw the heading of the letter. So, like any normal person would, she read the letter. Hoo-boy! The way Stacy told it, that letter made it sound like I hated her guts.

Anyway, Stacy (in deep shock!) folded the letter back into my diary and was just putting my diary back under my pillow, when I walked in on her.

Remember how I followed her downstairs, and how I caught Denny coming out of my room when I went back up there? Well, guess what? He must have been in there to snatch the letter back so I wouldn't see it and put two and two together. He had something behind his back, but I was too upset to be bothered with him. I really wish I *had* bothered, because it was quite obvious now that the thing he was hiding behind his back was that stupid letter!

The terrible twins must have figured that they'd cause the row-to-end-all-rows between Stacy and me. They must have thought they'd win the Strawberry Jam Revenge War at a stroke. And they nearly had, too, until we worked out what had really happened.

Remember I said right from the start how I

have the world's worst brothers? Do you believe me yet?

The question was: how were we going to pay them back?

Pippa got her notepad out again, to scribble down possible revenges.

'It has to be something so terrible that they won't dare to try and get back at you again,' Stacy said. 'Something unspeakably, unbelievably, unutterably awful!'

'How about we try the old Parcel-to-Timbuktu routine on 'em?' Fern suggested.

We all looked at her. The old *what* routine?

'You trick 'em into climbing into a big old trunk,' Fern explained. 'Then you drop the lid on them and padlock it shut. Then you can chain it up, just to be on the safe side. And then you mail it to some place way out in the middle of nowhere, like Timbuktu, and it's, like *Sayonara, twins!* See you in twenty years!'

'Don't bother writing that idea down, Pippa,' I said.

'Don't worry. I wasn't going to,' Pippa said. 'But, listen up, guys. Before we decide on the appropriate punishment, we need to be totally, utterly and completely *certain* that Denny and Bob are the culprits.'

'I already am!' I said.

'We must have proof!' Pippa insisted. 'We

don't want to do something awful to the twins and then find out that it was all down to . . . uh . . . to . . . um . . .' Pippa's voice trailed off.

'Yes?' I said. 'Go on. *Who?* Who else would do something like that?'

'The Phantom Poison Pen Prankster!' Pippa said. We looked at her. 'C'mon guys, it's *possible*,' she insisted. 'There might be some nut out there who sneaks into people's houses and leaves computer-written poison pen letters.'

'How would he get in?' Fern asked.

'The guy could be a professional house-breaker,' Pippa said.

'How would he know about Cindy and me?' Stacy asked.

'He could be a part-time Peeping Tom,' Pippa said. 'He could have been sneakily monitoring your every movement for, like, the past six months.'

'Uh, why would he bother to do that?' I asked.

'Who can dare to guess the strange and bizarre things that go on in the brain of a criminal mastermind?' Pippa intoned. 'He's probably a crazed and warped outlaw genius.'

'Or just *crazed and warped*, period,' Stacy said. 'Like *you*!'

'There's no such person as the Phantom Poison Pen Prankster!' I said. 'It was Denny

111

and Bob. And if you need proof, I'll get you some *proof*!' I gave Pippa a very determined look. 'And *then* we kill 'em!'

The important thing was to catch Denny and Bob off guard. If they knew we had figured things out, it might give them time to cover their tracks.

I had an idea how I might get some proof. If the twins had been really smart, then they would have erased all traces of the letter on the computer. I was kind of relying on the fact that my twin brothers weren't quite as smart as they thought they were!

When I got home later that afternoon, I made out like I still wasn't talking to Stacy.

Dad was in the utility room, surrounded by heaps and piles and towers of stuff from the garage. He was busily sorting and labelling and pricing everything for the yard sale. He was convinced we were going to have the Yard Sale of the Century. Mom told me that at the rate he was working, we probably wouldn't be having the sale until *next* century.

Denny and Bob were kicking up a racket in the living room with their model racing cars. Excellent! Keep it up, boys! While they were busy crashing their remote-controlled cars into the furniture and the walls, and yelling 'Cheat!'

and 'Not fair!' at each other, I had the perfect opportunity to do a little detective work.

I wheeled the computer work station out of their room and along the hall into mine. I booted it up and got to work.

We each have a personal folder. I clicked on the twins' folder and searched through their files for something incriminating. I opened a few possible files, but I couldn't find the one with the letter in it.

Curses! They weren't quite as stupid as I'd hoped.

I opened the Recycle Basket. There was all kinds of junk in there. I scrolled down the list. Where was it? I was hoping they hadn't been clever enough to wipe it completely. I was just thinking I might need to open every single file just to be on the safe side when a particular title caught my eye: C-BUSTER. Hmm. C for Cindy, maybe?

I opened it.

Ha!

Dear Debbie,

Ways In Which Stacy Allen Stinks!

Stacy stinks in so many ways that I don't know where to start! Her feet really stink! When she takes her shoes and socks off in gym she stinks the whole place out! And when she comes over to stay, I have to hold my breath when she gets ready for bed because her feet stink so bad. Stacy stinks in other ways too. She has stinky breath. I need a gas mask to talk to her. She thinks she's so smart, but really, she is not smart at all. That mangy cat of hers is smarter than she is. (Her cat stinks!) I used to like her, but I don't like her at all any more. What I would really like would be for her to go away and never come back again. That would be good, because I do not want to be friends with her any more. I'm only pretending to be her friend. I am telling you this so that you can give me some ideas for how I can get rid of Stacy. I would like you to be my best friend now.

I must stop writing now, because I am expecting Stinky-breath to arrive here at any time now.

From Cindy

I could just imagine Denny and Bob laughing themselves silly over that letter. Well, boys, I thought, prepare to start laughing on the other side of your faces! Big sister is out to get you. And the mood I was in, they were going to be *got* in ways they had never even dreamed of!

First thing Monday morning at school, I filled the guys in on what I'd discovered. I had even printed out a copy of the 'evidence' to show to Pippa. Pippa is a real whale on justice, so I figured she'd want to actually see the letter.

'Yup,' Pippa agreed. 'This is proof, OK.' She read it again. 'Unless . . .'

I stared at her. 'Unless what?' I said. 'You're not going to start talking about the Phantom Poison Pen Prankster again, are you?'

I glared at her. Stacy glared at her. Fern gazed out of the window – she was probably fantasising about her observatory!

'No,' Pippa said. 'No, I guess not.' She nodded. 'OK, gang meet at morning break to consider appropriate punitive measures against the terrible twosome.'

'Duh?' Fern said.

'We have to come up with ways of getting even with Denny and Bob,' Pippa explained.

'Getting *even*?' I said. 'No way! I want them

crushed like the stinky little bugs they are! I want them squished into squishy little pieces! I want them bashed and mashed and mangled and stomped on and wrenched and –'

'Cindy!' It was Ms Fenwick, our class teacher. She had come up behind us without any of us hearing. She stared at me in astonishment. 'Cindy, really, what language to use! What on earth are you talking about?'

'Oh . . . um . . .' I blushed bright red. 'The . . . uh . . . the . . . uh . . .'

Stacy jumped in to save me. 'We were just talking about the opposing team in our next basketball game,' she said quickly. She looked around at us. 'We're gonna stomp 'em, huh, guys?'

'We sure are!' Fern said.

Ms Fenwick looked at us. 'Yes, well, I'm glad to see you all so enthusiastic, girls, but I don't really think bashing and mangling and stomping and squishing will be necessary, hmm?'

'No, I guess not,' I said. I gave her my best 'nice-person' smile, just to prove I wasn't really the kind of basketball player who'd bash and mangle and stomp and squish the opposing team.

Ms Fenwick walked over to her desk and began registration.

Of course the really *big* news in class that

morning was the fact that I had been invited to appear on *My Real Best Friend. Everyone* watches that show. Everyone was real impressed! People kept asking me when I was going to be on TV, and I had to keep telling them I didn't know, but I'd put a notice up on the bulletin board when it happened, so they could all tune in!

Of course, my classmates were kind of surprised that I'd chosen Fern as my partner. I heard people asking Stacy why she wasn't going to be on the show with me. She spun them a line about stage fright and how she got cotton-mouth and panic attacks every time someone pointed a camera at her. Good old Stacy! I knew deep down she would have loved to be on the show.

Only one person came across like a total sour-puss. Betsy-Jane Garside. She's our class big-head. You know the type: her mom's car is bigger than your mom's car. Her allowance is twice as much as everyone else's. She has three hundred pairs of shoes in her closet. That kind of thing.

Well, she came sidling over to me.

'Cindy, that's really great about *My Real Best Friend*,' she said, sounding like she meant the exact opposite. She smirked at me. 'Of course, you do know how these shows work, don't you?' She was using her most irritating whiny-know-all voice.

'What do you mean?' I asked.

She smirked like a smirk-monster from the planet Smirk.

'They always invite more teams along than they're actually going to use,' she said. 'The rest just get told "thanks, but no thanks" when they get to the studio.' She simpered at me. 'Still, not to worry, huh? I'm sure you and Fern will be one of the lucky teams.'

And with that she slithered over to her own desk.

I glared at her.

What the heck was she talking about? The letter said I'd be on the show. What did Betsy-Jane Garside know about it? A big, fat *nothing*, that's what!

I forgot all about Betsy-Jane.

I guess I didn't learn a whole lot that morning. I had a repeating daydream in which I was on live TV, playing basketball with my brothers' heads. It was terrific! I ran down the court with Denny or Bob's head in possession. Bounce, bounce. Thro-o-ow. Whack off the back-board! Sco-o-o-o-ore! Ye-e-e-eay, Cindy! Cin-deee! Cin-deee!

Stacy, Pippa, Fern and I got together again at

morning break.

'Has anyone come up with any good revenge ideas for the twins?' Pippa asked.

'You bet!' Fern said. 'I have the whole thing worked out! We hide in the bushes out in front of Cindy's house, right? With *water* hoses. Then one of us knocks on the door. When Denny and Bob answer, we all turn on the hoses full power and squirt the little squirts right into the middle of next week!' She grinned. 'They won't even know what hit 'em!'

I stared at her. 'I don't know where to begin telling you what's wrong with that idea,' I said.

Fern frowned at me. 'Such as?'

'Well, for a start, there are no bushes in front of my house,' I pointed out. 'Secondly, where do we get the water supply from to power four hoses? There's only one outdoor tap, and that's around the back of the house. Thirdly, how do we make sure the twins answer the door? And fourth, how do we hose them down without squirting a whole lot of water in through the front door and all up the hall?'

Fern pondered for a moment. Then she looked up and grinned. 'Yeah, but *apart* from those things, what's so bad about it?'

That's Fern for you!

'Cindy,' Pippa asked me, 'have you come up with anything?'

I told them about my basketball fantasy. 'Or it would work with bowling or volleyball or football, too,' I said. I sighed. 'But I guess Mom would be mad at me if I actually killed them.' I shrugged. 'She's kind of strange like that.'

'I think we should ignore them,' Pippa suggested. 'That would be the civilised way of punishing them. We shouldn't talk to them for, say, two months.'

'We never talk to them, anyhow,' Stacy said.

'There is that,' Pippa admitted.

'I don't *want* to be civilised about this,' I said. 'I want to be totally uncivilised.'

'I have an idea,' Stacy said. 'Turnabout is fair play, yeah? So, I think our revenge should be something to do with a *letter.*'

'A letter from the FBI telling your folks that Denny and Bob are aliens!' Fern said, helpfully. 'Like that film – *The Village of the Damned*. Have any of you seen it? It's really neat. You see, these aliens come to a small town and – '

'Meanwhile, back on planet earth!' Stacy interrupted. 'I was thinking maybe that Denny'n'Bob could be sent a letter from a pretend new Four Corners baseball junior team. It could be called "The Four Corners Rockets" or something like that. We could print up a really convincing introductory letter on a computer. It could tell them that their names have been put forward to take part in try-outs for the team. We could make up a time and place when they have to attend, yeah? And then we send them to a totally fictitious address!'

'Stacy, that's brilliant!' I said with deep admiration. 'That's just so totally perfect! They're both nuts about baseball. They'll jump at the chance of being in a team.' A fiendish idea popped into my head. 'But we shouldn't send them to an address that doesn't exist,' I said. 'I know *exactly* where we should send them!'

I did, too! It was something I remember having seen advertised recently around town. The *perfect* time and the *perfect* place.

We agreed to get together at Pippa's house that afternoon after school to put the letter together.

That just about did it for morning break.

But I had one other problem on my mind.

I looked unhappily at Fern. 'I think we need to talk,' I said to her. 'Really seriously.'

'Sure,' she said. 'What about?'

'*My Real Best Friend*,' I said. 'Look, I really, really like you, Fern. But . . . well, I just don't think we're going to make it as a team.'

She stared at me. 'You want us to pull out?'

'Uh . . . no . . .' I said. 'Not exactly. I'd like you to . . . uh . . . think about . . .' I sighed. 'Gee, Fern, this is really difficult. The thing is, and I know this is a lot to ask, but I'd like you to think about stepping aside to make way for Stacy.'

An awful silence descended. Stacy looked anxiously at me. I could tell she was feeling as uncomfortable with this as I was. But what was I supposed to do? Let's face facts: inviting Fern to be my team-mate had been a mistake. I knew it. Fern must know it. And the TV audience were sure going to know it if we appeared together.

'I see,' Fern said after a few moments.

Pippa gave her a sympathetic look. 'I can see Cindy's point,' she said gently. 'And Stacy *is* Cindy's best friend.'

Fern nodded. 'Yeah, I can see that,' she said. She smiled at me. 'I guess we don't make the best team in the whole universe,' she said. 'You're right, we need to set things up differently.'

I breathed a sigh of relief. Fern wasn't always that reasonable, and I had to admit she had good cause to hit the roof this time.

'Pippa and I would make a great team,' Fern said.

'Yes, you sure would,' I said. 'Hey, maybe

My Real Best Friend will come near here again soon, and then the two of you could apply.'

'Excuse me!' Fern raised two hand, forefingers extended upwards. 'I didn't mean Pippa and I would make a good team *next time*,' she said. 'I meant Pippa and I will make a good team *this* time. My name's on that application form alongside yours, Cindy. I don't see why I should miss out on an appearance on TV just because you and Stacy have patched things up.' She pointed at me. 'I think *you* should step aside and make way for Pippa.' She smiled. 'I think Pippa and I should be on *My Real Best Friend*, that's what I think!'

I was speechless.

Was she kidding? I stared at her with my mouth open. No. No, she wasn't kidding. Fern really meant for me to drop out of the TV show to make way for her and Pippa.

Gahhhhh!

13

'No way!' I said. 'Never! Not in a million, trillion years!'

It was lunchtime. We were in the cafeteria. We were sitting at our favourite table over in the far corner by the window. We were having a nice, friendly discussion. Not!

'Fern has a point,' Pippa said to me. 'Why should she lose out?'

'Because if the two of us go on TV together,' I explained patiently, 'we're going to blow it big time!'

'I agree,' Fern said. 'But Pippa and I stand just as good a chance of winning as you and Stacy. *More* of a chance, maybe, because Pippa is a total brain-box.'

'Stacy's not exactly dumb!' I said. 'She's as smart as Pippa any day.'

'Oh, really?' Fern said. 'Spell "Mississippi", Stacy!'

'Why?' Stacy retorted. 'How would *you* know if I got it right?'

'She can't do it!' Fern crowed.

'I can, too,' Stacy said. 'But they're not going to be asking us to spell M, I, double S, I, double S, I, P, P, I, are they? Anyhow, Cindy and I know each other a whole lot better than you and Pippa.'

'I don't think that's true,' Pippa said. 'We know everything there is to know about each other!'

'Oh yeah?' Stacy said. 'Fern? What's Pippa's favourite book?'

'*The Phantom Tollbooth*,' Fern said.

'Totally correct!' Pippa crowed. 'See?'

'I *ought* to know it,' Fern muttered. 'She keeps on *reading* the darned thing to me every chance she gets. Princess Rhyme and Princess Reason! Huh, if I'd been Milo, I'd have gone in there with a fully armed Chinook helicopter and blown those Demons of Ignorance to itty-bitty pieces!'

'OK,' I said to Pippa. 'So, what's Fern's favourite book?'

Pippa laughed. 'That's a trick question!' she said. 'Fern doesn't have a favourite book. She doesn't *like* books.'

Fern nodded happily. 'It's true,' she said. 'I don't get books at all. I mean, what's the point in reading stuff that some person just *made up*? I started reading a book once. It was about this

125

Canadian boy and a wolf that he met out in the woods. And I was really getting into it. I thought it must be really neat to have a pet wolf. So I said to my dad, "Hey, Dad, can I have a pet wolf?" And he said no, no one has pet wolves! And I said, but the boy in this book I'm reading has a pet wolf! And he said, but that's not a true story; that never really happened. And I thought, well, right, if some author guy is going to tell me lies, he can just go and get lost, as far as I'm concerned. So I dumped the book in the trash.'

The three of us looked at Fern for a few moments after she'd finished.

I couldn't think of a single, solitary thing to say. I was just really, really glad that we weren't going to be on television together! I mean, can you *imagine*?

'The point is,' Pippa said, looking at me. 'Fern has as much right to have a place on *My Real Best Friend* as you do. Her name is on the application form, after all.'

'But I sent off the original application to the TV network,' I said. 'If it wasn't for me, *no one* would be appearing on the show!'

'Exactly correct!' Stacy said. 'Cindy *has* to be on the show. It'd be the unfairest thing in the world if she wasn't.'

'You would say that,' Fern grumbled, ''cos

that means you get to be on TV, too, if you're her team-mate.'

'That's not why I said it at all,' Stacy declared. 'I don't care about being on TV.'

'Fine,' Fern said. 'So we go back to the original plan. Me and Cindy.'

'No!' I wailed. 'We'll lose! We'll be hopeless!'

'Then let me and Pippa appear,' Fern said.

'I've just thought of something,' Pippa said. 'What if the people who put the show together insist that the two people whose names are on the application form have to appear together? See what I mean? They may not let us change people around at all.'

'Easy-peasy,' Fern said to Pippa. 'I tell them I'm Cindy Spiegel, and that you're Fern Kipsak. Who's to know?'

'Everyone who's ever met us!' Stacy said. 'They'll all see us on TV!'

'But it'll be too late by then,' Fern said. 'We'll have won and it'll all be done and finished with.'

'It won't be too late for them to cancel the tickets to Hawaii,' Pippa said. 'And to publicly denounce us as cheats and frauds.'

'Rats!' Fern said. 'Wait!' she added. 'I have a better idea! They wouldn't be so strict that they'd stop one of us choosing a new partner if

127

our original partner was too ill to appear. All
we have to do is to tell them that Cindy has the
mumps or appendicitis or a peanut stuck up
her nose. I could bring Pippa in as my substi-
tute partner, and everything would be just
dandy!'

'A peanut stuck up my nose?' I said dazedly.

Fern shrugged. 'It could happen. I got a
peanut stuck up my nose when I was a little
kid.' She grinned. 'They had to take me to hos-
pital to get the sucker out of there! No one in
their right mind would want to appear on TV
with a peanut jammed up their nose.'

I've said it before, and I'll say it again: Fern
is insane!

'I'm not going to fake some stupid illness just
so you and Pippa can appear on the show,' I
declared loudly. I tapped my chest. 'I'm going
to be on the show because the whole thing was
my idea. Now *I'd* like to have Stacy as my partner.' I looked at Fern. 'Will you act like a reasonable, sane human being for once, and back
down so that Stacy and I have a chance of winning a dream vacation?'

Fern gave me a long, slow look.

'Nope,' she said.

'What we have here,' Pippa said, 'is what we
call, in legal circles, an *imposs*.'

'A what?' Stacy asked.

128

'An *imposs*,' Pippa repeated. 'It means no one is prepared to back down.'

'Are you sure *imposs* is the right word?' Stacy asked.

'Of course,' Pippa said loftily. 'It's called an *imposs* because it's *impossible* to reach an agreement.'

(Note: I thought you might like to know that Stacy found out later on that the word Pippa meant was *impasse*. It means exactly what she said it meant, except that it's not short for 'impossible'. Apparently it's a French word. It means 'stalemate' and 'deadlock'. Which was about dead right for the position we were in! Anyway, back to the story. End of Note.)

'So, where does that leave us?' Stacy asked. 'How about pistols at dawn to decide?'

'I'd prefer missiles at midday,' Fern said with a grin. 'Whoosh! Blaaam! Instant decision!'

'Ahem!' Pippa coughed. 'What we need,' she said, 'is an independent person who will be able to judge both cases on their merits. Fern will put her side of things, and Cindy will put hers. And then this independent person will make a ruling on who should appear on the show, and everyone will have to go along with the decision!'

'That sounds OK,' Stacy said cautiously.

'What third person were you thinking of, Pippa?'

'I hadn't gotten that far,' Pippa said. 'But it has to be someone who isn't bothered either way.' She looked around the cafeteria. 'Someone like . . . uh . . . Rachel Goldstein.'

We all looked over to the table where Stacy's sister, Amanda, was holding court with the three other Bimbos: Rachel, Natalie and Cheryl. Rachel Goldstein is a tall, gangly ginger-haired idiot with a walnut for a brain.

'But she's an imbecile!' Stacy protested. She looked around, too. 'How about Andy Melniker?' Andy is a boy in our class. We don't have a whole lot to do with him, but then we don't have a whole lot to do with any of the boys in our class. They're mostly complete dorks!

'He's a flake,' Pippa said. 'He's out of his mind!'

We all looked at him. He was two tables away with a couple of his mates: Peter Bolger and Larry Franco. I kind of like Andy. Pippa was right, he is a complete flake, but, as you already know, some of my best friends are pretty flaky, so what can I say?

'Do you think he'd do it?' I asked.

'I'll go ask,' Fern said. She got up and made her way over to the table where Andy and Peter and Larry were sitting. She spoke to Andy. The three boys looked around at us in interest.

Stacy gave a little wave. Pippa rolled her eyes.

Fern came back and sat down.

'So?' I asked. 'What did he say?'

'He said he'd do it.' Fern grinned. 'So I invited him around to Pippa's house after school this afternoon.'

'So, it's decided, then,' Pippa said solemnly. 'Listen, guys, we have to make a pact, here. We have to agree to go along with Andy's ruling, no matter what we privately think of it. Agreed?'

We all agreed.

After all, if Andy had even just one sensible brain cell in his head, he'd have to choose Stacy and me. It was so totally obvious!

I just really hoped that Andy did have one sensible brain cell in his head. The way his brain seems to work sometimes, it wouldn't surprise me if he came up with the decision that I had to appear with Stacy's cat as my partner! Or that Fern should go on the show with a *penguin*.

Andy can be pretty off the wall!

14

We met Andy after school and the whole bunch of us headed over to Pippa's house. Mrs Kane was home already, so she fixed us some sandwiches and drinks before we went up to Pippa's room to begin what Fern called 'The Final Conflict!', the test to decide once and for all which two of us should appear on TV. Stacy and me, or Pippa and Fern.

'Who's the pin-up?' Andy asked Pippa, staring up at one of Pippa's posters. He'd never been to Pippa's house before.

'Virginia Woolf,' Pippa said. (She was a writer. A dead one. Pippa's really into dead writers. Don't ask why.)

'Oh, right,' Andy said. 'I think I saw her on TV last weekend.' He nodded. 'Great voice. Lousy song.'

'Wha-at?' Pippa screeched. 'She was a *writer*, you idiot! A really great writer!'

Andy grinned at her. 'Oh,' he said. '*That* Virginia Woolf.'

132

'OK,' Stacy said before Pippa had the chance to strangle Andy. 'Here's the list of questions we prepared.' She handed the list to Andy.

It was divided into two sections. 'Favourites' and 'What Would She Do If . . .' The 'Favourites' were things like, favourite teacher, favourite movie, favourite bubble bath, and so on. The 'What Would She Do If . . .' questions were things like: 'What would she do if you borrowed her favourite skirt without asking and spilling barbecue sauce all over it?' or 'What would she do if she was abducted by aliens?' (Take a guess who thought that one up!)

Pippa had figured out how the contest should be run. I would sit with Pippa. Stacy would sit on the other side of the room with Fern. Andy would say, 'Here's a question for Stacy.' Then he'd read out the question. Stacy would whisper her answer to Fern. I'd whisper my answer to Pippa. Then Fern would repeat Stacy's answer aloud. Then Pippa would tell everyone what I'd actually said.

If the answer Stacy gave was way-off, then our team would get a zero. If it was close but not exactly right, we'd get one point. If it was spot-on, we'd get two points.

It worked like this.

Andy: 'Question for Pippa. What would

Fern do if she saw some big guys bullying a little guy?'

Pippa's whisper to me: 'She'd march over and stop them.'

Fern whispers to Stacy.

Stacy, out loud: 'Fern says she'd wade in and slaughter 'em!'

Fern: 'Too right, I would!'

Me: 'Pippa said Fern would march over and stop them.'

Andy: 'That sounds about right. I guess they'd stop bullying the little guy once Fern had slaughtered them. Score two to Pippa and Fern.'

Andy worked his way through the 'Favourites' section. I really hoped Pippa would be asked to name Fern's favourite colour! That would put Stacy and me two points ahead, no problem!

'Question for Pippa,' Andy asked. 'What is Fern's favourite colour?'

Yessssss! Who-hoo! We'd been level-pegging so far. This was where we'd shoot into the lead.

'She has a different favourite colour every day,' Pippa whispered to me, while Fern was whispering to Stacy.

'Fern says she changes her mind about her favourite colour all the time,' Stacy said out loud.

I repeated what Pippa had whispered to me.

'That's close enough for me,' Andy said. 'Score two for Pippa and Fern.'

Rats!

'Question for Cindy,' Andy said. 'What is Stacy's favourite movie?'

My mind went totally blank. What was Stacy's favourite movie? I could think of at least half a dozen that she had really raved about. I looked at Stacy, tying to read her mind. She stared back at me.

Cindy to Stacy, Cindy to Stacy – what's your favourite movie of all time?

It had to be an animal movie. Stacy is nuts for animal movies. But was it *Brigands of Beaver Creek* or *Tiger, Tiger* or *The Wilderness Trail* or *what*?

Think, Cindy! Think!

'*The Wilderness Trail!*' I whispered to Pippa.

Stacy whispered to Fern.

'Stacy says her favourite movie is *All the Way*,' Fern said.

Argh! *All The Way* is a movie I bought Stacy on video last Christmas. It's about two girls who are best friends. When the movie starts off the girls are both ten years old. The movie shows how they grow up and have families and get divorced and move to other parts of the country and stuff, but how they still stay really good friends. And then one of them gets ill.

135

The other one drops everything and rushes over to nurse her until she finally dies right at the end of the movie. The surviving friend goes for a walk along the beach at sunset. It's so *sad*, but it's great at the same time that they were there for each other all through their lives.

'Cindy said *The Wilderness Trail*,' Pippa said. She sounded pretty cheerful that I'd gotten the movie wrong. I guess I couldn't blame her.

'Score of zilch for Stacy and Cindy,' Andy said. 'Pippa and Fern lead twenty-four points to twenty-two.'

'I thought you'd go for an animal movie!' I said to Stacy.

'I picked *All The Way* because you bought it for me!' Stacy said. 'I thought you'd think I was thinking that I'd chosen one that I thought you thought I liked!'

I thought about an answer to that, but it just made my brain hurt.

'We'll do better next time!' Stacy said.

'Yeah,' I agreed. I sure hoped so!

I secretly crossed my fingers that Pippa and Fern would foul up. (Yes, I know you should-n't wish for people to make a mess of things, but I figured these were exceptional circum-stances. I mean, we're talking about a TV appearance, here.)

'OK,' Andy said. 'Question for Fern. What

would Pippa do if she was using her computer and the hard drive crashed?'

Pippa whispered to me. 'I wouldn't touch anything,' she said. 'I'd call the service people and ask their advice.'

Sure, that would be the *sensible* thing to do. But, you know, Pippa doesn't always do the *sensible* thing. Sometimes she does the *totally insane* thing. Like, I could almost imagine her prodding around inside the back of the computer with a screwdriver!

Fern whispered to Stacy. Stacy grinned and nodded in agreement.

'Fern says she'd probably haul the back off and poke around in there to try and see what was wrong,' Stacy said with a big grin. 'And she says the Pippa Jinx would probably kick in around about then, and she'd wind up blowing the house to bits!'

'I would not do any such thing!' Pippa yelled. 'What do you think I am: insane?'

'Excuse me,' Fern said. 'What about that time my personal stereo broke down and you had it in, like, five hundred pieces? I had to take it to a repair shop in the end, and even the guy in there couldn't put it back together again.'

'That was completely different,' Pippa said. 'You just lost us our lead, Fern!'

Fern looked at her. 'Some people need to be a little more honest about themselves!' she said. 'What did you tell Cindy you'd do?'

'She said she wouldn't touch anything –' I began.

'Hah! I bet!' Fern interrupted. 'That'll be the day!'

'And she said she'd call a service engineer,' I continued.

'Yeah,' Fern said with a big grin. 'But not until the computer was in twenty million teensy-weensy little pieces all over the floor!'

'Score a big fat *nothing* for Pippa and Fern,' Andy said. 'You guys are level again.'

I gave Stacy the thumbs up sign and she nodded. We were back in contention.

Andy carried on asking the questions, and we carried on answering them. Every now and then one or the other of us would get something wrong. But within a couple of questions, the scores always seemed to even up again. It was beginning to look like Stacy and I knew each other exactly as well as Pippa and Fern knew each other. That wasn't what I wanted to find out at all!

Andy would occasionally throw us a really weird question: 'Question for Cindy. What would Stacy do if she was carried off one morning by a giant bat?'

'We never wrote that!' I complained.

'Yeah, I know,' Andy admitted. 'But your questions are all kind of ordinary, know what I mean? I thought I'd try livening things up a little.'

'Answer the question!' Fern said. 'There's nothing in the rules that says Andy has to stick to the questions we made up.'

'OK!' I said. I whispered to Pippa. 'She'd probably convince the bat to turn up for "show and tell" at school.'

Stacy whispered to Fern.

'Well?' Andy asked.

'Stacy said she'd make friends with the bat and use it to ride to school every morning,' Fern said.

Darn! Close but no prize!

'And she'd ask it if it would be prepared to make an appearance for "show and tell" ,' Fern finished.

'Yesss!' I yelled, punching the air. 'That's just what I said she'd say!'

Two points to us!

Another of Andy's crazy questions was: 'What's Fern's favourite flavour of soap?'

Pippa looked at Fern for a few moments and then whispered 'Chocolate,' to me.

I looked at her. She raised her eyebrows and shrugged.

Fern whispered to Stacy.

'Fern said chocolate,' Stacy announced.

I nearly fell through the floor! Wow! Pippa and Fern must be able to read each other's minds. They almost *deserved* to win with answers like that!

I did say *almost*.

Ten questions on, and we were still level.

Andy looked at his watch. 'I have to go, guys,' he said. 'My mom said to be home by six.'

'You can't just *go*!' Stacy yelled. 'We're still tied!'

'I guess that means you should *all* appear on the show,' he said.

'No! No! No! No! No!' Pippa said. 'You're not getting out of here until you make a decision.'

'OK,' Andy said. He looked around at all of us, as if he was thinking really hard. 'I choose Stacy and Pippa!' he said suddenly as he ran for the door.

'Get him!' Fern yelled as he flew out into the hallway, laughing like an idiot.

He outran us. The last we saw of him, he was racing down the street like a bullet. He was still laughing when he got to the corner and vanished.

We trooped back to Pippa's room.

So much for Andy Melniker, the Great Judge! We'd wasted the entire afternoon, and we were no nearer coming up with a solution to our problem.

'You know,' Stacy said. 'Andy might have a point.'

'Yeah,' Fern grumbled. 'Right on top of his head!'

'No listen,' Stacy continued. 'He said maybe we should all appear on the show. Now, let's be honest, guys. He's right, isn't he?' She looked at Pippa. 'You and Fern know each other just as well as Cindy and I do. We all deserve to be up there on the stage.'

'Excuse me,' Pippa said. '*My Real Best Friend* doesn't allow teams of four. I mean, Max and Margarita aren't idiots. They're going to see the four of us up there, and someone is going to do a quick head count and spot the problem. They're going to notice that there's too many of us.'

'I have an idea,' Stacy said. 'I think we should all turn up at the studios. We can explain the situation to them, and let them decide who should go on the show.'

I blinked at her. 'I'm sorry, but that doesn't sound like too much of a brilliant idea, Stacy,' I said. 'What if they're too busy to bother deciding? What if they tell us all to get lost?'

'They can't do that,' Fern said. 'They need at least two of us for the show. I think Stacy's right.'

I though about this. If we carried on trying to find a winning team between ourselves, the chances were that we'd end up throwing dice! I'll level with you, I didn't want my chances of appearing on *My Real Best Friend* to be decided that way!

But if we agreed to let the TV people choose between us, the odds were pretty heavily stacked in my favour. After all, I sent the original letter. I set the whole deal up. Fern was just my chosen partner. Chosen by me (in a moment of madness!). So, I figured, the TV people would have to pick Stacy and me.

I know this was a really selfish way of thinking, but it wasn't like I'd come up with the idea. I was just going along with the others, right?

That was it. Decision made!

We'd all go along to the shoot on the day, and the people who run the show would have to choose whether to take Stacy and me or Fern and Pippa.

And, if you want to go with the smart money, I suggest you put your money on the team whose names begin with S and C.

15

The next thing we did that afternoon was to plan out and print up a letter to send to Denny and Bob. We decided to go along with Stacy's 'Four Corners Rockets' baseball team try-outs. The finished letter looked really great. It told how recruiting scouts had been secretly observing school kids from all over town, and how the twins had been chosen because they were so talented.

I told the guys my idea for where we should tell them to go for the try-outs. I also told them what was really happening that day at that place. We all fell about laughing. We were going to get Denny and Bob but good! I'll fill you in on what happened a little later on.

Meanwhile, all that next week I was climbing the walls waiting on a reply from *My Real Best Friend*. People at school kept asking me where the programme was going to be taped. When it was going to be taped. When it was going to be on TV.

In the end I put a note up on the board:

Cindy does not have any new information
about My Real Best Friend *right now.*
So, please stop asking.

The week crawled on, and I had to keep reading the letter from the TV people to convince myself I hadn't dreamed the whole thing. Then it happened.

I received a phone call on Thursday evening. From *them*! At last! I nearly passed out as Mom handed me the phone.

It was a nice-sounding young woman who told me her name was Amy. 'Do you have a pen and some paper handy, Cindy?' she asked. 'Because I'd like to give you the details, OK?'

'Sure!' I squeaked excitedly. I was trembling. I could hardly hold the pen. This was it! This was real! I was about to appear on TV!

Eeeeeeeeeeek!

I scribbled down everything she told me. The show was going to be recorded in the Petra Wilson Hall in the Oswald Zitter Complex right smack in the middle of Mayville. I needed to be there with my 'best pal' at midday on the Saturday after next. I was to make myself known to the stewards, and they would give me a special back-stage pass.

'Good luck Cindy!' she said. 'Do you have any questions?'

'Yes,' I squeaked. My brain was spinning around in my head. It was really going to happen! In nine days' time I would be in front of the cameras. 'I folks my come can please with friends?' I blathered down the phone.

'I'm sorry?' Amy asked.

'My folks,' I said. I took a deep breath and grabbed a hold of my brain with both hands. It slowed down and I managed to say what I meant. 'Can I bring my parents and friends?'

'Oh, yes, of course,' Amy said. 'I'm sorry. I forgot to tell you. Each nominated team is given an allowance of six tickets. You can invite more people along than that, but they may not be able to get in. We get a pretty large audience, Katie, I have to warn you.'

'I'm Cindy!' I said. Katie? Who the heck was Katie?

'Oh! I'm dreadfully sorry,' Amy said. 'Cindy, of course! I've been calling people up about the show all afternoon. I guess my mind is beginning to wander. Anyway, I'm looking forward to meeting you, Cindy. Best of luck!'

'Thanks,' I said.

Maybe I should have heard alarm bells starting to ring about then, but I didn't. The question I guess I should have asked myself after that call was this: as there are only ever *four* teams on *My Real Best Friend*, why did Amy need to be on the phone to people all afternoon?

Maybe I should have remembered what Betsy-Jane had told me.

Rats! I hate it when smug, big-headed show-offs are right about stuff!

Oh, I meant to tell you: the letter addressed to 'Dennis and Robert Spiegel' arrived on Wednesday. In case you're wondering, Dennis and Robert are Denny and Bob's real names, but no one ever uses them. I just thought the whole thing would seem more official if we used their full names.

They went for it like a ton of bricks!

'The Four Corners Rockets Want YOU!'

After that the twins strutted around the house like a pair of champion, prize-winning roosters. Their heads swelled up even more when they called around all their friends and found out no one else that they knew had been invited along to try out for 'The Four Corners Rockets'. They kept on and on about how they'd get on the team, no problem. Boy, were they ever in for a big fall! If they had been a little less big-headed about it, I might even have felt sorry for them. But they weren't, so I didn't! Especially when I remembered what they'd done to deserve it!

'I really hope you do get picked for the team,' I said to them at one time, much to their astonishment. 'I'm sure you're *exactly* the kind of people they're looking for!' If only they knew!

One of the funniest thing was how they said they had figured all along that they were being watched by a talent scout. They even said they'd seen him talking to their gym teacher at school.

It was my opinion that a week on Saturday was *never* going to come! Time had gotten all fouled up, and no matter how hard a person wished, that weekend always seemed a million years away!

Everyone was buzzing in our class at school. People asked about tickets to the show, and I had to tell them about the limited allowance. Some people said they'd come along anyway, but most decided to watch the show when it was broadcast. Andy Melniker asked about his ticket for helping us out. I reluctantly agreed that he could have a ticket.

Gradually, minute by long minute, Saturday got closer.

I hardly slept at all on that final Friday night.

And I was so hyped-up on Saturday morning that my mom said she should attach weights to my feet to keep me from shooting up into the air and exploding like a Fourth of July firework!

We all piled into the car and headed for Mayville.

Denny and Bob were pests as ever, and I only just avoided getting melted chocolate all over my best dress because they insisted on fighting over a squishy Hershey bar in the back of the car.

The street layout system in Mayville was a total nightmare. I leaned anxiously over Mom's shoulder as she drove around and around. I showed her my watch. It was ten minutes to twelve. We had to be there in ten minutes!

'I know!' Mom said. 'We'll get there. Don't worry.'

Don't worry? How could I not worry?

We hit the entrance to the parking lot for the Oswald Zitter Complex at four minutes to twelve. I left the rest of them to park the car. I asked the guy at the gate which way to the entrance for the Petra Wilson Hall. He gave me directions and I ran like crazy.

I know it sounds kind of silly, but I had this feeling that something bad would happen if I didn't get there by twelve noon. You know, kind of like Cinderella and the stroke of midnight. I imagined someone barring my way to the entrance and saying: 'Sorry, you didn't make it in time!'

I whooshed around a corner and nearly banged right into a long line of people. At the front of the line I could see a couple of people with clipboards. They looked like the stewards that Amy had told me I should report to.

I searched the line of people for anyone I knew. There were a couple of faces from our school, but mostly it was people I didn't recognise, until I caught a glimpse of Stacy and Fern, standing to one side with their folks, way down at the front of the line.

Fern saw me. She waved frantically and called me forward.

I felt really important as I marched right up past the line of people who were only part of the audience. ''Scuse me,' I felt like saying. 'Contestant coming through!'

'Where are your folks?' Fern asked me.

'Parking the car,' I explained. I said hi to Fern's mom and dad and to Stacy's parents. Stacy's dad was carrying baby Sam but he was asleep, so I guess he wasn't too over-awed by the whole occasion.

'Where's Amanda?' I asked Stacy.

'Cheerleading,' Stacy told me. 'She said to say "break a leg".'

'Huh?' I asked.

'It's a good luck thing that people in show business say to each other,' Stacy explained. 'When you go on stage they say "break a leg", meaning that they hope nothing goes wrong.' Stacy shrugged. 'Don't ask me why.'

'It doesn't sound too lucky,' I said dubiously.

'Yeah,' Fern added. 'And knowing Amanda, she probably really meant it!'

'Have you been given your back-stage passes yet?' I asked them.

'No, we were waiting for you,' Stacy said.

'And Pippa,' Fern said. 'If she's late, I'm gonna kill her.'

As if on cue, Pippa came running up. 'My mom's parking the car,' she panted. 'We got lost.'

'Us too,' I said.

'OK!' Fern said. 'We're all here.' She grabbed my arm and propelled me towards the nearest steward. 'Go tell them the plan, Cindy.'

'Oh! Thanks!' Fern nearly catapulted me right into a young woman with a bright yellow T-shirt and a clipboard.

She smiled at me. She had a huge, gleaming

white smile. It was as if she had light bulbs in her mouth. 'Hello, can I help at all?' she said.

'My name's Cindy Spiegel,' I told her. 'I'm going to be on the show.'

'That's just fine, Cindy!' she said. 'Just give me a moment.' She flipped over a page on her clipboard and ran her pen down a list.

'Cindy Spiegel!' she said cheerfully. 'Here you are!'

'I sure am,' I said.

I saw her pen flick as she ticked my name. 'And you're with . . . uh . . . Fern Kipsak, right?' She smiled brightly at me. 'Is she here yet?'

'Uh, yes,' I said. 'But the thing is . . .'

'Yes?' She looked down at me and all of a sudden I wasn't at all happy about trying to explain our big plan to her.

'Uh . . .' I glanced over my shoulder. Stacy's folks were chatting with Fern's folks. 'Uh . . . hold on a moment.' I beckoned to Fern. She came over. Stacy and Pippa followed after her. The steward gazed expectantly at us.

'Fern,' I mumbled. 'Do you want to explain?' I said lamely.

'Sure thing,' Fern said. She looked up at the steward. 'It's really simple,' she said. 'The fact is that I really like Cindy, but she's not really my *best* friend, yeah? Not, like, my *best friend* in

151

the whole of the known universe. My real best friend is Pippa, here.' She pointed to Pippa and Pippa nodded enthusiastically. 'Pippa Kane,' Fern said as if she expected the steward to write Pippa's name down on her list. 'K. A. N. E.' Fern spelled. 'With a K, not a C, right?' The steward showed no sign of being about to write anything down, so Fern carried on with the explanation.

'Now,' she said, 'Cindy here is best friends with Stacy.' She pointed to me and then to Stacy.

'Hi,' Stacy said.

'Hi,' the steward said back, but I got the feeling her smile was getting just a little strained.

'So,' Fern said. 'You can see how it is, right?' The steward looked back to Fern. 'The thing is,' Fern continued, 'we thought maybe you people could choose between us.' The steward stared blankly at her. The smile was definitely fading now.

Fern looked at her for a few moments.

'I'm sorry?' the steward said.

Fern lifted her hands, forefingers stretched up. 'OK, too complicated,' she said. 'That's fine. No problem. Maybe I didn't explain it too well.'

'Excuse me,' Stacy interrupted. 'What Fern is trying to say is that we've tested ourselves and we've come out just about totally *even*, so we thought maybe you could decide for us?' She looked up at the puzzled steward. 'Could you do that for us?'

'I want to have Stacy as my team-mate,' I said.

'And I want to have Pippa,' Fern added.

The steward looked from me to Fern and then back to me again. She consulted her list. 'Cindy Spiegel,' she said, 'partnered with Fern Kipsak. That's what I have written down here.'

'Yes, we know that,' Pippa said. 'But Cindy only put Fern down as her best friend because she'd had a fight with Stacy. But now they're best friends again. But that doesn't mean Fern should have to give up her chance of appearing on TV, does it? So we thought maybe you people could decide who gets to be on the show. See?' She gazed hopefully up at the steward. 'Cindy and Stacy, or me and Fern.'

The steward looked at us for a very long time.

'Wait here,' she said at last. 'I'll go get Valerie.'

She scuttled off in through the glass doors of the building.

'Is anything wrong?' Mrs Allen called over to us.

'No,' Stacy called back. 'Everything's fine.'

'She didn't seem to understand what we wanted,' Fern said, staring after the steward. 'She must be a little slow.'

A couple of minutes later the steward came back out with a power-dressed woman with short black hair and a face that looked like it had been *lifted* once too often. She had a smile like a shark having a bad-fin day. She had a bigger clipboard than the first woman, and it had more documents on it. I figured that meant she was more important.

'This is Cindy,' the steward said to her.

'Hello, Cindy, I'm Valerie Sachs,' said the woman. 'I'm the producer of *My Real Best Friend.*' I remembered her name – she'd signed that first letter. 'Tamsin seems to think there's a little problem.' She glanced at Tamsin as if she thought Tamsin was the problem. 'Now then, would you like to tell me? I'm sure it can all be sorted out very easily.'

I took a big breath. 'I'd like Stacy as my team-mate,' I said. 'But Fern doesn't think that's fair, because I put her down as my team-mate on the form. But that was before I made up with Stacy. But Fern says she has as much right to be on the show as I do, and she'd like to appear with Pippa, here.' I took another breath. 'The thing is, we can't choose, so we . . . uh . . . hoped you'd . . . uh . . .' My voice trailed off. Valerie Sachs was flicking through the forms on her clipboard. ' . . . uh . . . sort of . . . choose . . . for . . . us . . .'

'Yes,' Valerie said. 'I see. Here we are.' She pulled a form out. She showed it to me. It was my application form. 'This states quite categorically that you would like Fern Kipsak to appear as your team-mate,' she said. 'I'm very sorry, but our rules are quite specific.' She flipped the form over. There was a whole lot of tiny writing on the back. I hadn't paid it any attention before. It was the kind of writing you'd need a microscope to read. 'Section C sub-section 2, paragraph 1 states quite clearly that any changes to the team as specified in part B, 4, of the application form, must be cleared by our office forty-eight hours before the date advised for the taping of the programme.' She smiled her sick shark smile. 'Except in exceptional circumstances of illness, bereavement or other unforeseen and unforeseeable particular cases, that is.' She shook her head. 'I'm afraid, from what you've told me, Cindy, your situation isn't covered by any of those circumstances. I'm afraid I'm powerless to help you. There's nothing I can do about it.'

There was a short silence. I looked at Pippa. If anyone was going to have understood what all that stuff meant, then it would be Pippa.

'So,' Pippa said slowly. 'You mean it's gotta be Cindy and Fern? Cindy and Fern or . . . uh . . . no . . . one?'

Valerie Sachs nodded. 'Yes, I'm afraid so.' She shark-smiled at me and then at Fern. 'If you two girls would like to come through, I'll take you along to where all the other teams are waiting.'

'Yeah, but –' Fern began.

'I just –' I said.

Pippa shook her head at us. 'It's the rules,' she said. 'No swapping partners at the last minute.'

'Come along!' Valerie Sachs herded Fern and me ahead of her into the building.

Fern gave me a resigned kind of grin. 'I guess we'll just have to do our best, huh?' she said. 'It could be worse.'

'I guess so,' I said. I looked at her. 'How could it be worse?'

'You could have gotten mad at all of us and put Betsy-Jane down as your team-mate,' Fern said.

I nodded. Yeah. I guess it *could* have been worse, at that.

Valerie the Shark shooed us across the foyer and down a corridor. She opened a door and kind of *hooshed* us into a room with a great big table running down the centre. A dozen or so kids were sitting in chairs around the table, nibbling from plates of snacks, drinking sodas.

'Peter, this is Cindy and Fern,' Shark Woman said. 'They're the last, I think.'

'Thanks, Valerie,' said a tall, thin, smiling man with a pony-tail. Shark Woman disappeared. Fern and I were offered drinks from bottles on a side table and told to sit wherever we liked.

There was quite an atmosphere in the room. I mean, you could tell the kids were nervous and excited and strung out. I couldn't figure why there were so many of us. Including Fern and me, there were enough pairs to make up eight teams.

Maybe they were going to tape two shows at once?

And then we found out the truth.

'OK, everyone,' Peter said, standing at the head of the table. 'I want to tell you a few things about how *My Real Best Friend* works. As you can see, there are a lot more people here than we need for the actual show. Now, this is something we always have to do in case people drop out at the last minute, or in case someone gets a real bad attack of the nerves and decides they can't go through with it.' He smiled around at us. 'Not that any of you guys look the nervous type,' he said with a grin.

157

My stomach turned over. I had a real bad feeling about what he was going to say next. I had the real bad feeling that Betsy-Jane Garside had been right all along.

'Now,' Peter continued, 'I have here the list of teams that will actually be appearing on the show. But if your names aren't on the list, I don't want you to feel bad about it. We have great consolation prizes for everyone today, so no one's going to go away empty-handed!'

He picked up a sheet of paper.

'OK,' he said. 'These are the teams who will be appearing on this afternoon's show.'

I crossed my fingers.

'Bill and Ivan.'

I crossed my toes.

'Harvey and Russ.'

I crossed my legs.

'Katie and Kirsty.'

I crossed my eyes.

'Janis and Sarah.'

My heart sank like a stone. We hadn't been picked! I couldn't believe it. All that effort and we hadn't even been picked to appear on the show.

Fern sighed. 'I guess it could be worse,' she said softly.

I looked at her. 'How?' I moaned. 'How could it possibly be worse?'

She gave me a feeble grin. 'We could have broken a leg. Like Amanda wished on us,' she said.

16

Peter called another woman in and the four teams who had been picked to appear on the show were taken out.

The rest of us sat there like a bunch of pathetic no-hopers. I sneaked a look at the other rejects. Some of them looked stunned, like they couldn't quite believe it. Others looked blank. A couple looked like they were trying not to burst out crying.

Believe it or not, the thing that bothered me most right then was the thought of having to face Betsy-know-all-Jane! Boy, she'd milk this for all it was worth.

'OK, guys,' Peter said. 'Now I know you must all feel really miserable that you're not going to appear on TV.'

'Too darned right!' Fern muttered.

'But not one of you is going to be allowed to leave this room until I see a smile on all your faces!' Peter said.

I stared at him. He was going to make us

smile? Was he kidding? Well, good luck, mister, if I ever smiled again, it wasn't going to be for a couple of years, at least.

He turned and picked up a big cardboard box off the floor. He dumped it on the table. 'OK,' he said. 'Let's see what we have in here to put the smiles back on a few gloomy faces.'

The box was just stuffed with consolation prizes.

First out of the box were fifty-dollar vouchers for Milligans Department Store. Milligans is the biggest and the best store in the whole of Mayville. We got a fifty-dollar voucher each. Fern and I looked at each other like we couldn't quite believe it.

Next out come a bunch of really cute teddy bears, each with a little T-shirt on. The T-shirts were yellow and said 'You're My Real Best Friend'. We were given a bear each, along with full-size *My Real Best Friend* T-shirts just like Peter and the stewards were wearing.

Then we all got buttons and stickers and a special gift pack of *My Real Best Friend* candies. There were *My Real Best Friend* writing sets and a huge big wall poster for each of us of Max and Margarita. We were given sunglasses in a *My Real Best Friend* case and *My Real Best Friend* baseball caps.

I was beginning to think: Hey, maybe not appearing on TV isn't so bad after all!

Finally, Peter gave each of us a complimentary family season ticket to Global Village Theme Park. Global Village is a totally brilliant place with dozens of rides and fun stuff to do.

Fern and I stared at the tickets and then at each other. Global Village was kind of an expensive place to visit – and now we could go there every weekend for six months if we wanted to!

This was working out almost better than appearing on TV.

We were given *My Real Best Friend* carrier bags to load all our goodies into, then we were taken into a room behind the big hall where the show was going to be taped. Max and Margarita were there. They were really great. They chatted with all of us and gave us autographed pictures of themselves as well as a video each called *My Real Best Friend – Oops! Don't Broadcast That!* The videos were outtakes and bloopers from previous shows. They told us these weren't even available in stores!

We were then shown to special VIP seats in the front row of the audience. The hall was filled with people by then. The stage set was ready and there were cameras and banks of lights all over, as well as lots of technicians scuttling around like frantic ants.

Of course, the first thing Fern and I did once we were in there was to go find our folks and fill them in on what had happened.

'Oh poor you,' my mom said when I told her we hadn't been picked for the show.

'You've gotta be kidding!' I said, grinning. 'Take a look at all this!' I showed them my bagful of goodies.

'Just so long as you aren't too disappointed,' Dad said.

I smiled. 'Well,' I said, 'I guess it would have been great to appear on TV, and all that, but it's not like the end of the world that we weren't picked. And a dream vacation would have been great, too, but a six-month pass to Global Village is even better, because it'll last a whole lot longer!' I waved down at the stage, where the contestants were lining up ready for the show to start. 'When all those guys have left of their vacation is a bunch of pictures, I'll still be visiting Global Village!'

'Not fair!' moaned the twins. 'What do we get?' Huh, like they *deserved* anything!

'It's OK,' I told them. 'It's a family ticket to Global Village! We can all go.'

'Every week!' Denny yelled.

'Twice a week!' Bob howled.

'We'll see,' Mom said.

Right then someone on the stage called for quiet.

The show was about to begin.

We managed to fix it so Stacy and Pippa could come and sit with us down at the front. Boy, seeing a show live is a whole lot different to watching it on TV, I can tell you! For a start, the show took over an hour and a half from start to finish, even though *My Real Best Friend* is only a half-hour programme on TV. A whole lot of stuff goes on that you never see.

Like, the girl called Katie tripped over a step when she came on the stage, and she went sprawling on her face. So they had to stop and tape the thing again. The out-takes video was filled with stuff like that.

We had a really great time, and after the show was "wrapped" (that's what they call it when the taping finishes. They say, "OK, people, That's a wrap!") the whole bunch of us – Fern and her parents, Stacy and her folks, Pippa and her mom, and me and my family – all went out for a pizza together. It was a riot!

So there you are, that's the story of how come I never got to appear on *My Real Best Friend*. But like Fern said, things could have been a whole lot worse.

Yeah, like, for instance, I could have

appeared with Fern and we could have been a total disaster in front of millions of TV viewers!

Oh, in case you were wondering, Kirsty and Katie won the dream vacation – two weeks in New England. Not bad, huh?

Oh yeah, I have one last little thing to tell you.

The little matter of my revenge on my pesky kid brothers!

'Shhh!' I hissed to Fern. 'They're coming!'

The four of us were hidden out of sight behind the changing lockers in the Springdale Sport Centre.

It was the Sunday after our big day out in Mayville, and our revenge plan on Denny and Bob was about to take place.

Pippa giggled and I had to *shush* her.

Stacy nudged me as the doors to the changing room opened and Denny and Bob came in.

'Are you sure this is the place?' Bob said, looking around. I ducked back. I didn't want to be seen just yet. Not *just* yet! There was total silence from the sport hall at the other end of the changing room. We had arrived there early to tell all the guys in there what we had planned and why my brothers needed teaching a lesson.

They had agreed to go along with us.

This was going to be sweet!

'Second floor, red room,' Denny read from the letter. 'Yup, this is it.'

'It's kind of quiet,' Bob said. 'Maybe they haven't started yet.'

'Let's go see,' Denny said.

They walked down towards the double doors that led to the hall.

Denny pushed the doors open. That was our cue. We slipped out of cover and crept up behind them.

There was the yell of a couple of dozen girls' voices from beyond the doors. Denny and Bob backed off in horror.

Through the open doors, we could see the whole line-up of the junior cheerleading squad, all in their little silver and blue rah-rah skirts, and all with their silver and blue pom-poms in their hands.

'It's the new recruits!' called their trainer. 'Come on in, boys, we've been waiting for you!'

'Gaagh!' Denny choked. 'Yerrrk!'

'Gruugh!' Bob gagged. 'Groooh!'

They turned to escape, and bumped right into Stacy, Pippa, Fern and me.

'Going somewhere, boys?' Fern asked in her best menacing voice.

'You don't want to miss out on all the fun,' I

said, spreading my arms out to bar their way. 'They've even had special little suits made up for you!'

A look of sheer panic went over the twins' faces.

'How do you feel about joining the Four Corners Rockets, huh?' Pippa laughed. 'Oh, I guess there was a typo on the letter you were sent. It's not a baseball team at all, it's a cheer-leading squad! But you can still join in!'

A few of the girls from the squad came running out into the changing room, yelling and laughing. They grabbed Denny and Bob.

The twins fought like crazy to get away while the girls tried to drag them into the hall.

Wow, talk about major panic!

The twins had almost been hauled right into the hall before they broke loose.

Whoosh! They bolted down the length of the changing room like a couple of ballistic missiles. I bet they'd never moved so fast in their lives. There was the final glimpse of horrified faces as they skedaddled down the corridor.

'Hey, do you think we embarrassed them?' Stacy asked.

Everyone laughed.

I dusted my hands together. 'I think it'll be a while before they mess with us again!' I said. I grinned at Stacy, Pippa and Fern.

They grinned back. We were a great team!

I thanked the cheerleading squad for their help and we headed down to the street.

'Who wants a sundae?' Fern said. Uncle Mac's Ice Cream Emporium was just across the road.

'Excellently excellent idea!' Stacy said. She linked arms with me as we made a beeline for Uncle Mac's.

I grinned at her and she grinned back at me.

I don't need to appear on a TV show to know who my real best friend is! Stacy Allen is my real best friend, and she always will be!

And there's more . . .

Stacy and Friends 3

My Sister, My Slave

When Amanda starts to become a school slacker, Mom is ready to take drastic action – pull Amanda out of the cheerleading squad! So the sisters make a deal; Stacy will help Amanda with her school work in return for two whole days of slavery. But Amanda doesn't realize that when her little sister's boss, two days means 48 *whole* hours of chores – snea-kee!

ISBN 0099263599 £3.50

Coming Soon

Stacy and Friends 5

Stacy
the Matchmaker

Amanda is mad that the school Barbie
doll, Judy McWilliams, has got herself
a boyfriend, and to make things worse
it's hunky Greg Masterson, the guy
Amanda has fancied for ages. Stacy
feels that it's her duty as sister to fix
Amanda's lovelife and decides to play
cupid and do a bit of matchmaking,
with disastrous results!

ISBN 0099263637 £3.50

Stacy and Friends 6

The New
Guy

Pippa's under pressure. It was bad
enough that her mom and dad went
and got divorced, but now it seems
that her mom's fallen for some geeky
new guy – called *Kevin*! Who needs
some meddlesome man around when
she and her mom were doing just fine.
It's down to Stacy and friends to make
sure that if Kevin's going to stay on the
scene not only is he a suitable suitor
for mom, but he passes the Pippa test
too!

ISBN 0099263645 £3.50